THE LIBE[RTY MAN]

GILLIAN FREEMAN was born in Londo[n] honours in English literature and philos[ophy] in 1951 and afterwards worked as a cop[y] literary secretary to the novelist Louis G[olding] career of her own. In response to an advertisement placed by the fledgling literary agency of Anthony Blond, Freeman submitted the manuscript of her first novel, *The Liberty Man*, which went on to be published by Longmans and was one of the best-reviewed novels of 1955. By 1961, Blond had his own publishing house and wanted to publish a "Romeo and Romeo" novel with working-class gay protagonists; the result was *The Leather Boys*, published under the pseudonym of Eliot George. The book was well received and went into numerous paperback printings in the US and UK during the 1960s and '70s before Gay Men's Press reprinted it in 1985 as part of its *Gay Modern Classics* series; it was also adapted for Sidney J. Furie's Golden Globe-nominated 1964 film, for which Freeman wrote the screenplay.

Freeman's other novels include *The Leader* (1965), a disturbing "what if" story about a Fascist's rise to power in Britain; *The Alabaster Egg* (1970), a historical novel whose title refers to a gift from the gay King Ludwig II to his lover that later finds its way into the possession of a young woman in Nazi Germany; *Nazi Lady* (1978), the fictional diaries of a woman of the Third Reich; and *An Easter Egg Hunt* (1981), the tragic story of a young girl in Edwardian England who disappears from a boarding school on Easter Sunday. More recently, Freeman's *His Mistress's Voice* (1999) and *But Nobody Lives in Bloomsbury* (2006) have been published by Arcadia Books.

In addition to her novels, Freeman has written a number of screenplays, including *That Cold Day in the Park* (1969) and *I Want What I Want* (1972). Her nonfiction works include the influential study of pornography *The Undergrowth of Literature* (1967) and *Ballet Genius: Twenty Great Dancers of the Twentieth Century* (1988), the latter co-authored with her husband, the novelist and ballet critic Edward Thorpe. Freeman also wrote the scenario for Sir Kenneth MacMillan's immensely successful ballet *Mayerling*, which premiered in London in 1978 and which has since entered the repertoires of ballet companies all over the world.

Gillian Freeman and Edward Thorpe have two daughters and live in London.

Cover: The cover reproduces the jacket art of the 1955 first edition, published by Longmans, Green and Co. The illustration is by Ley Kenyon (1913-1990), best known today for his role in the "Great Escape" from Stalag Luft III prison camp during the Second World War, which was the basis for the 1963 film *The Great Escape*.

BY GILLIAN FREEMAN

FICTION

The Liberty Man (1955)*

Fall of Innocence (1956)

Jack Would Be a Gentleman (1959)

The Leather Boys (1961)*

The Campaign (1963)

The Leader (1965)*

The Alabaster Egg (1970)

The Marriage Machine (1975)

Nazi Lady: The Diaries of Elisabeth von Stahlenberg, 1933-1948 (1978)

An Easter Egg Hunt (1981)

Love Child (1984) (as Elaine Jackson)

Termination Rock (1989)

His Mistress's Voice (1999)

But Nobody Lives in Bloomsbury (2006)

NONFICTION

The Story of Albert Einstein (1960)

The Undergrowth of Literature (1967)

The Schoolgirl Ethic: The Life and Work of Angela Brazil (1976)

Ballet Genius: Twenty Great Dancers of the Twentieth Century (1988)

SCREENPLAYS

The Leather Boys (1964)

That Cold Day in the Park (1969)

I Want What I Want (1972)

The Day After the Fair (1986)

* Published by Valancourt Books

GILLIAN FREEMAN

THE LIBERTY MAN

With a new introduction by
EDWARD THORPE

VALANCOURT BOOKS

The Liberty Man by Gillian Freeman
First published London: Longmans, 1955
First Valancourt Books edition, January 2014

Published by Valancourt Books, Richmond, Virginia
Publisher & Editor: James D. Jenkins
20th Century Series Editor: Simon Stern, University of Toronto
http://www.valancourtbooks.com

ISBN 978-1-939140-80-7
Also available as an electronic book.

All Valancourt Books publications are printed on acid free paper
that meets all ANSI standards for archival quality paper.

Set in Dante MT 11/13.6

INTRODUCTION

So much has changed in London—indeed in Britain—since Gillian Freeman's first novel, *The Liberty Man*, was originally published in 1955. Socially, demographically, economically, technologically, politically, it is an entirely different scene.

London's East End,[1] familiar to Freeman's main characters, Derek and Freda, has long since lost the scars of wartime, the bomb-sites overgrown with weeds, the narrow streets lined with working-class homes lacking bathrooms and indoor lavatories. In their place are high-rise tenements and, nearby, a group of glittering skyscrapers filled with bankers and hedge-fund managers. The electric trolley buses were soon changed for diesel vehicles and homosexuality between consenting adults has not been a crime since 1967.

London's West End, the department stores, theatres and fashionable restaurants, has fewer of the sleazy bars that Derek and his shipmates frequented although, if one chooses to look for them, their counterparts exist; today's demi-monde is just that much more sophisticated. Even more pertinent, sailors in uniform have disappeared: nowadays they go ashore smartly dressed in whatever is the current fashion. The navy has stopped the centuries-old custom of dishing out a daily tot of rum and the service itself has diminished to a small part of what it was in Derek's day. London is, now, the centre of a multi-cultural society that would astonish not only Derek and Freda but also their respective parents. Even so, the class differences that ruined Derek's and Freda's affair still obtain, more pronounced, more complex than fifty-odd years ago.

Today, it would be extremely unlikely for a service man, whose family live on a modern council estate, to take up with a woman from the Home Counties.[2] A supply teacher in Mile End, like Freda, would more likely be domiciled in that locality, perhaps be a member of one of the several ethnic communities that make up that part of London.

There remains the social barrier of accent. Derek's Cockney[3] has broadened into what is now called Estuary English[4] as opposed to RP—Received Pronunciation—of the middle-classes. The shortened vowels, the glottal stops, the dropped aitches, the missing final consonants of Estuary English, together with a concomitant vocabulary, are an immediate indication of a person's background and mode of living unlikely to be shared with a member of the middle classes.

How was it, then, that Freeman, whose own background was liberal, cultured middle class, could write so authoritatively about the inhabitants of London's East End and, more surprisingly, the occupants of the Royal Navy's lower decks?

Coming down from University with a degree in English Literature and Philosophy, Freeman had already had some short stories published in literary magazines and journals. To enlarge her career as a writer she decided to embark on a novel. Following that commonplace advice to any would-be novelist, Freeman utilised material from personal experience and charged it with her imagination. A short period of supply-teaching in the East End was followed by an equally short period as the literary secretary to a distinguished English novelist who happened to be gay, with a pronounced penchant for the company of sailors. Freeman had had, therefore, the experience of teaching obstreperous cockney girls as well as being witness to a constant stream of partying matelots. She was intrigued by their hard-drinking, easy-going, insouciant temperament and quickly became familiar with their naval slang, their off-duty habits, their preferences and interests. This contiguity, lower deck and her own background, resulted in *The Liberty Man*.

The raw material of the book was expertly moulded into an intrinsically doomed affair. One's heart aches for Derek, who glimpses a lifestyle more interesting, more satisfying than his own, and Freda, whose nascent sexuality is stimulated by a handsome young sailor, to find some way towards a permanent liaison. It is not to be: external forces, the class differences of the period, are too strong for a happy ending within the time-frame of a three-week leave.

Freeman not only pinions her protagonists with unerring accuracy but deftly etches in subsidiary characters such as the brusquely practical Miss Carstairs, the school headmistress, and the impoverished gentility of Mrs. Gibson-Brown, Freda's landlady. Freeman also illumines each scene with some telling detail, from the dried sugar clinging to a spoon at an all-night coffee-stall to the smudged nail varnish on the fingers of a school girl; from the peeling poster hanging from a boarded-up shop-front to the Italianate façades of elegant South Kensington.

When the novel was first published one leading London critic wrote, *"The Liberty Man is an altogether astonishing first novel for a young woman to have written."* That judgement still stands today.

EDWARD THORPE
London

October 29, 2013

EDWARD THORPE toured extensively as a boy actor and later graduated from the Royal Academy of Dramatic Art. He was dance critic for the *London Evening Standard* for twenty-five years, lectured extensively in the UK and US, and is the author of five books on dance and two novels.

NOTES

1   East End: A poor part of London; indigenous home of Cockneys, severely bombed during World War Two.
2   Home Counties: The semi-rural counties that form the outlying areas of London often referred to as "the stockbroker belt".
3   Cockney: Inhabitants of London's East End, mostly poor, tough, resilient and endowed with a mordant, fatalistic sense of humour.
4   Estuary English: The speech patterns of that part of the County of Essex bordering the northern shore of the River Thames estuary.

THE LIBERTY MAN

FOR

EDWARD THORPE

When the wind was out to sea
And she was taking leave of me,
I said "Cheer up, there'll always be
Sailors ashore. . . ."

Traditional Song

The First Week

I

SIGNALMAN Derek Smith closed his suitcase by sitting on it and
went over to give Able Seaman John Cooper a hand with his
uniform. On the crowded mess-deck there was great activity. Men
struggled into their skintight jumpers, adjusted their collars, shined
their shoes, and stowed their gear in readiness to go ashore. The
white ellipses of freshly blancoed hats looked like rows of dinner-
plates, and socks and underwear hung, waiting to be packed, from
the tangle of overhead pipes. Pin-ups were reverently taken from
the insides of lockers and preserved between the pages of photograph albums. H.M.S. *Dragon* was home after ten months 'foreign'.

Already the ship seemed strange and alien. Voices echoed, cases
and hold-alls littered the shiny steel deck. The men, suddenly, were
no longer a part of *Dragon's* crew, a compact and co-ordinated
team, but individuals doing individual things.

Johnnie Cooper carefully tied his white lanyard.

"Not long now, eh, Smudge?" he said. "A few hours and we'll be
home."

Together they joined the long line queueing for leave pay.
Through the inch-thick glass of the porthole the sky was veiled
with drizzling rain.

"Just like Capri!" called out some wit.

"Could do with one of them vino-shops now," said Derek to the
fellow next to him. It was the National Service rating from his
mess. He had been to a public school and they called him Fauntleroy, but he wasn't unpopular.

"And how!" said the boy. He added politely, "What are you
doing this leave?"

"Goin' to 'ave a drink," said Derek, "as soon as I can get my
'ands on one."

"I meant, are you going home?"

"Yes. Are you?"

"Yes. I expect my mother will be meeting me at Waterloo and we'll go home together. Where do you live?"

"You wouldn't know where," said Derek sharply. "Down London Docks."

Conversation flagged a moment, then: "Have you got a girl?" Twelve months on *Dragon* had taught Fauntleroy the chief interests of his fellow sailors.

"Sort of!" Derek wasn't forthcoming. He'd almost forgotten what she looked like this time, but he didn't doubt she'd be round that evening to give him plenty of chance to remember.

They had reached the top of the queue now.

"Don't blow it all tonight," said the paymaster automatically; "remember you've got three weeks." He had started it off as a joke and now felt compelled to say something to each of them.

Derek and Fauntleroy waited for Johnnie.

"Remember you've got three weeks," the paymaster said. No one ever answered him.

The three of them went along to the Master-at-Arms' office, collected their leave passes and travel warrants and descended again to the mess-deck. There they sat about restlessly on long wooden benches until two metallic pipe-notes sounded through the loud-hailer system, followed by the command from the Quartermaster: "Liberty men, fall in."

There was a scraping of feet, and a wild scramble for the companionway.

"Come on," called Derek over his shoulder, "there won't be a train for another hour. The pubs'll be open before then."

They moved through the rapidly emptying ship, lugging their belongings up the steep ladder.

"Blimey!" gasped Johnnie as they reached the upper deck, "I've 'ad about enough of this lark already. The eighth of May, and nothing but bleedin' rain."

Drops of moisture clung to the freshly painted upper-works and the paying-off pennant stretched from the fore-mast like a strip of bandage unwinding itself the full length of the ship. Destroyers and cruisers seemed to have been placed in the oily harbour water and forgotten, while further outstream the flat-topped silhouette of an aircraft carrier was like an enormous stage abandoned by a concert party on a rain-soaked sea-front. Low clouds swept in with the south-west wind, making the town seem as grey as the naval craft, and the only colour to be seen was the bright reds and blues of the women's coats on the dockside as they waited with flasks of tea to welcome home the men. They had been singing popular songs before the crew had begun to disembark, and the spirit of excitement, coupled with the feeling of uncertainty, made it all not unlike a wartime homecoming. As the men began to come down the gangway, some hurrying, alone, others in boisterous groups of twos and threes, they were greeted with frantic shouts and waving and a great deal of hugging and kissing.

It was somehow embarrassing to see the men you knew so well, shared your watches with, ate with, went ashore with, indulging in these sentimental embraces, becoming fathers and husbands and sons. Three weeks and they'd be normal again, free and swearing, lining up for the daily tot of rum, no longer the possessions of these coloured-coated, arm-holding women.

"I could have told my mother to meet me here, if I'd thought," said Fauntleroy. "What a pity."

"No good 'avin' 'er 'angin' about in the rain," consoled Derek. "Come and 'ave a wet with us." Fauntleroy didn't really want a drink then, but he didn't like to seem unsociable. Actually, he had fallen easily into this naval ritual of making a drink the prime pleasure in life, whether it was in the refreshment room at Waterloo or a sleazy dive in Singapore.

They passed through the gate, and the customs men, keeping a look-out for the *Dragon* cap tally, let them go through without bothering to check them.

They turned for a last glimpse of the ship, and felt a little sentimental.

"Well, that's that," Johnnie summed up for them all. "Could do with that wet, Smudge."

The three of them made their way into the town. Opposite the Compasses the man with the hamburger stall looked as if his arm was beginning to ache on its swift, repeated journeys with the mustard spoon. He popped the flat sausage cakes into the rolls, squashed the roll-tops down till they looked like grinning mouths with sausage-meat tongues, and handed them over on their greasy squares of paper to the line of eager matelots.

Inside the Compasses the bar was full. Glasses frothed and the three weeks' pay, plus victualling allowance, had begun its change of hands across the counter. Above the noise, the pub's parrot squawked incessantly.

"There's a nice welcomin' sight for you," said Johnnie, jerking his head towards the door. "Pompey Minnie waitin' for some poor bloke."

Pompey Minnie was sixty now, with two respectable daughters married in the town.

"My God," said Fauntleroy distastefully. "What a sight."

"I've seen worse," said a Chief Stoker coming up behind them with a pint in each hand. "She's all right in a dark room.

"Hallo, my love," he called. "How's life?"

Pompey Minnie tottered over to them. "Life's all right," she said. "What about a drink for an old friend?" She put a hand on his sleeve, the blue and red tattoo below her wrist incongruous against the rest of her aggressive femininity. "Staying a few days?"

"Not bloody likely," said the Stoker. "My old woman's waiting for me in Prestwick."

"Why not go tomorrow?" wheedled Minnie, "and have one last evening with an old friend?"

"What a harridan," said Fauntleroy. "She's like something out of a painting by Toulouse-Lautrec."

"'Oo's 'e?"

"A Frenchman, a cripple. He painted tarts and women in pubs."

"Oh, why didn't you say so?" Inwardly Derek was rather impressed. "You don't 'alf have your 'ead bunged up with a lot of rubbish," he said scornfully. "There's only one sort of picture I'm interested in, and you can't get those in England, neither."

"London train in ten minutes," shouted a sailor from the doorway. He was wearing his girl-friend's hat and his mates thought it very funny.

"Come on," said Johnnie, "let's get steamin'."

The platform was crowded, a frieze of creased bell-bottoms, freshly washed collars, shining shoes. Some of the men sat on cases and smoked, some slept, leaning against one another for support, a group passed round a bottle of whisky.

Walking self-consciously apart from the rest, two young officers wearing cloth caps and shabby tweeds talked earnestly as they threaded their way up and down, the drizzle blowing in on them from the edge of the roof.

The train twisted slowly between the platforms. *Dragon's* first leave party rose as one man and surged forward, laughing and shouting, helping each other with the luggage, commandeering one compartment after another. The platform was suddenly empty, there were faces at every window. An expectant stillness, and then the train moved off with an electric hum. Ahead lay London, and a long leave. Someone started to sing a bawdy song and others joined in, but the words tailed off into embarrassed laughter. Within half an hour most of *Dragon's* lower-deck crew were asleep. A couple of men were playing cards, the whisky bottle was still going, there was a little half-whispered conversation.

"Got a skylark up in Smoke. Want to come?" A skylark meant anything.

"No thanks. Got a date. Give us the bottle, Scouse. Don't drink the ruddy lot."

It was still raining when two hours later the Portsmouth train pulled in at Waterloo.

"Coming for a quick one?" asked Johnnie.

Derek shook his head. "No. I'm going 'ome." He pulled his case on to the platform and watched the huddle of blue thin out into the stream of civilian grey and brown.

"What about you, Faunty?"

But Fauntleroy shook his head too. "I must look for my mother. She's probably outside somewhere. Cheerio." In a second he was gone.

"So long, Smudge," Johnnie said.

"S'long, Johnnie. Be seeing you!"

They parted at the barrier and Derek started to make his way home to the East End.

He struggled down the escalator into the Underground, his eye caught by the advertisements for brassières, and the posters announcing the new films. On the platform, what with the people trying to get on, and the people trying to get off, it seemed a worse scramble than when they practised Action Stations on manœuvres.

At Charing Cross he forced his way out again and with growing irritation dragged his case up stairs and escalators to the Metropolitan line. Typists and business men, school teachers and clerks swept him along in a whirl of umbrellas and brief-cases and library books. This concentration of anonymous humanity made him feel lonely. If he was to be surrounded by lots of people they should be familiar, like his mates on the crowded mess-deck. These strangers, wrapped in the tight cocoons of their secret selves, gave him a sense of uneasiness. They were pushing against him, breathing on him, close as lovers, yet in a moment they would move away, never to be seen again.

At Aldgate East he managed to get a seat. At Stepney his carriage was almost empty. At Mile End he got out himself.

Coming out into the road he had a strange sense that he wasn't in London but on the promenade at Southsea. It was the empty spaces of the bomb-sites, the grey sky and the smell of rain that did it. A poster hung wet and peeling from a boarded-up shop-front. A gull wheeled overhead. At the Park Café the neon lights glowed, and turned the food in the window an unappetizing yellow. In between the fake cottonwool ice-creams Derek could see a negro eating a plate of fish and chips. He felt tired, and thought of going in for a cup of tea, but changed his mind and cut across the rough weedy ground that had once been the post-office to wait for a trolley-bus. The rush hour seemed to have subsided, or else people worked later in this part of the world. His bus came, the doors opened and closed with an automatic whirr, and he paid the fare that would take him to the end of his street.

Two or three girls he didn't recognize were lolling outside the newsagent's which was still open.

" 'Allo, Jack," called one of them, and the others giggled.

"'Ow many wives you left be'ind this time?" went on the girl, encouraged.

"Now then," said Derek, putting down his worn leather case, "'oo y' cheeking?"

"I know you," piped a pert little blonde with long ear-rings and a sweater through which her breasts showed like two small apples. "You're the one what goes with Maureen Lacey up at our flats."

So I am! thought Derek. He was conscious of feeling depressed at being labelled and docketed. "The one what goes with Maureen Lacey." He hadn't thought of Maureen Lacey for months, and all that time she'd been claiming him as her boy, her sailor.

"I suppose I am," he said, winking at the girl with the ear-rings, "but you know what sailors are."

The girls giggled again and Derek picked up his case.

"Be seein' you," he said. He walked off with a deliberate nautical roll and turned down a side street.

Jubilee Road, late Hanover Street, said the grimy board on Mrs. Harris's front wall. It all seemed smaller than he remembered, the houses narrower, the doors lower. The open-air feeling he had had at Mile End was gone. He wanted to walk down the middle of the road, the pavement was so cluttered with dustbins and push-chairs.

Mrs. Hayman was standing on the doorstep of number twenty.

"Well, if it isn't young Derek," she called across the empty street. "'Ad a good time?"

"Yes thanks," Derek shouted back. "Smashin', thanks."

"Your Mum know you're back?"

"She will in a minute."

He turned in to number twenty-three. In the untidy patch of garden the forget-me-nots straggled in the beds, the eight white sea-shells flaunted their share of London soot. Dad got fits and starts of doing the garden and this obviously wasn't one of them. The front door was still not painted either. "A nice green," his mother had said she wanted. He went in and got his bearings a minute in the dark hallway. At once he was aware of the familiar smell he had forgotten. His mother was a clean woman but there always seemed to be this smell of damp cardboard and cooking.

He pushed open the kitchen door, and with the odd feeling of not having been away more than a day or two, his eyes took in the brown patterned wallpaper, the clothes horse bearing the Monday wash steaming in front of the fire, above the mantelpiece the mirror with green and orange glass panels on either side.

His mother was setting the table.

" 'Allo, Mum," he said.

She turned, still holding a bread-knife in one hand, smoothing down her apron with the other.

"Derek!" she said. "You did give me a turn!" He could tell how pleased she was to see him.

" 'Allo, Mum," he said again. He gave her a quick peck on the cheek. "I've got you one of them little raffia baskets from Italy."

"You're in time for tea," cried his mother. "Your Dad's only just got in!"

Mr. Smith came out of the scullery drying his hands.

" 'Allo, son. 'Ow did the old girl be'ave?" He meant the ship. He had been in the Merchant Navy and there was evidence of his travels in most of the rooms.

"Where's Joan?" Derek asked, wanting his whole family gathered together for his homecoming.

"She's settin' 'er 'air," his mother told him. "Going out with 'er boy tonight." She suddenly remembered. "Maureen know you're back?"

"She probably does by now," said Derek, recalling the little blonde outside the shop. He felt constricted by this lack of freedom. Joan's boy. His girl. Thank God for the navy.

"Let's 'ave some tea," he said, "I'm starvin'."

His mother pulled another chair up to the table and began to cut into the pie.

"Steak and kid," his father said. "You come 'ome on the right day."

His sister came into the room, her hair done up in a turban, and her hands held in front of her like a begging dog, because she had just painted her nails. She was not quite fifteen, seven years younger than he was. They had always been friends, gone to the same school, and as a child she had ridden in his orange-box cart and stood up for him in his back-street fights. Now he was a sailor she was very proud of him.

"'Allo, kid," said Derek.

"'Allo, Derry. You're a one, not writin' to tell us."

"You know me. Anyhow, Mum likes surprises, don't you, Mum?"

"I don't know so much as I do," his mother sniffed. "I don't 'ave much choice, do I?"

"This calls for a celebration," said Mr. Smith. "Let's 'ave a couple of bottles of wallop."

"Never say no to a wet," grinned Derek. All at once he remembered his presents for them. 'Rabbits' they called them in the navy.

"Shall I get the things I brought you?" he asked. He always enjoyed this part of coming home. It was tangible evidence of his having been to strange foreign places.

"Ooh yes," giggled Joan. "I wouldn't not have a sailor in the family for anything, would you, Mum?"

But Mrs. Smith was embarrassed. Whenever her husband or children gave her presents she at once felt she didn't deserve them. Her manner became brusque and ungrateful, and she found the act of accepting acutely awkward.

"There's plenty of time!" she snapped.

"Come off it, Mum," reproved Mr. Smith. He turned to Derek. "Brought us back some interestin' little mementos from foreign parts?"

Mr. Smith's own "mementos" were for him the crystallizing of particular experiences he had had as a merchant seaman. The lump of coral in the sitting-room grate had trapped in its brittle coruscations the memories of dazzling Pacific beaches. The elephant's foot door-stop recalled the day when, happily drunk, he and his mates had brawled in the jostling bazaars of Bombay. He frequently recounted these experiences in the local on Saturday nights but, to his wife, his inarticulate, beer-blurred descriptions failed to make his curios anything more than so many things which had to be dusted.

Derek flung back the lid of his suitcase and began to rummage through it.

"'Ere you are, Joan. Got them in Nice for you. What all the French girls are wearin'." He gave her a pair of scarlet, rope-soled beach sandals. "And some stockin's."

"'Ere, Dad." He handed his father what looked like a piece of pumice stone. "One of them stones from Pompey."

"From Pompey?" Mr. Smith looked puzzled.

"Yeah. You know. The one in Italy where everythin' got buried all them years ago. I went along with Fauntleroy, a brainy bloke in our mess."

Mr. Smith fondled the stone lovingly. "All them 'undreds of years," he said. "Can 'ardly credit it."

"Eat your tea, for 'eaven's sake," nagged Mrs. Smith, seeing her turn was coming.

"'Ere you are, Mum," said Derek, giving her the black raffia bag. He always brought her presents she couldn't use. Slanting sunglasses from the Riviera, silk scarves, or nylons.

"Oh, it's lovely, but I couldn't use it," cried Mrs. Smith, seizing the bag, tears coming into her eyes. "You shouldn't 'ave spent your money on me, Derry. I don't like it."

"Go on, Mum," said Joan. "You know you're pleased. What you got for Maureen, Derry?" She was contemplating a possible swop.

"Blimey!" said Derek, "I 'aven't brought 'er nothin'."

"Give 'er my bag," Mum suggested. "I don't want it. You got to give your girl something."

"You can't give away the present your boy 'as just give you," said Mr. Smith firmly, going back to his tea, the Pompeii stone in front of his plate. "It's not right."

"I'll see what I got, shall I?" offered Joan.

"I never said she was my girl," began Derek.

But the situation was already out of his hands. Joan and his mother were searching through the dresser drawers, finding half-empty bottles of nail-varnish, even a pure Irish linen duchess set that had been a wedding present twenty-eight years before.

"I know." Joan had an idea. "The necklace Dad got Mum in Greece. You don't mind, Dad, do you? She ain't never worn it."

"All in a good cause," said Dad philosophically, scraping his plate. "Your Mum never was one for trinkets."

The necklace, made of camel-bone, with a picture of the Acropolis on alternate beads, was located and examined.

"And 'ere's a nice paper servi to wrap it in," cried Mrs. Smith, producing a white square with a beaming Father Christmas in the centre.

The excitement was over now. Derek poured out the beer for his father and himself, and the four of them settled down to eat again. They hadn't really much to say to each other.

"Your Auntie Ellen died last month," said Mr. Smith.

"We got a new teacher in our class," said Joan at the same time.

"Tell us where you bin," urged Mum. "Give us the pickle, love, will you?"

"Well," said Derek. "We went all round the Med. Istanbul, Capri, Gib. You know, the usual Cook's tour."

This meant nothing at all to his mother, but she liked to take an interest in what he did.

"You goin' to get engaged to Maureen, this leave?" asked Joan. "All the girls at the club think you're goin' to."

"They'll have to have another think then, won't they?" he said. "Blimey, I only even wrote 'er once."

The front-door bell rang.

"She 'asn't wasted much time, 'as she?" said Mr. Smith with a wink. "Go and let 'er in, Derek."

Angry still, he went to the front door and opened it, but at the sight of Maureen his anger disappeared. She wasn't as pretty as the little blonde, but she was small and neat and had brown curly hair. All his sexual longings, which had been sublimated and redirected these last weeks, swelled up inside him.

"'Allo, Maur!" he said.

"'Allo, Derek." She came into the hall and took off her mackintosh. "You're not still 'aving your tea are you? Rose Limage told me you was home."

"That the blonde?"

"Yes."

He wanted to kiss her, but was suddenly inhibited and opened the kitchen door instead.

"It's Maur," he said.

" 'Allo, Maureen," said Mrs. Smith archly. "It's a long time since we seen you."

" 'Ave a cuppa," invited Mr. Smith. "Or perhaps you'd rather 'ave a glass of beer? I know you girls."

"No thanks for both," Maureen said. "I just come round to see Derek. Rose Limage told me she see 'im this afternoon." She let her eyes rest tenderly on Derek for a moment. It was so romantic knowing a sailor. These last couple of weeks, since she'd had that lovely card from Nice, had been ever so exciting and worrying. If he didn't want her now she couldn't think how she'd face the girls again. She'd been wearing his photograph in her locket ever since he'd gone away.

"You 'ave a good trip?" she asked him, admiring his sunburned skin and crew haircut. She wasn't capable of deep emotion, but jealousy entered into this. "I bet you met some smashers ashore, didn't you?" There was an edge to her voice.

"Course 'e did!" said Mr. Smith. "Ever met a sailor what didn't?"

"It's the 'eart what counts," murmured Mrs. Smith reassuringly, feeling it up to her to say something. Maureen was a nice girl.

"Want to go up the Palais tonight?" asked Derek. He knew it was her favourite place and that she wouldn't go alone, and he was feeling touched by her devotion. He had just caught sight of his own face on the end of the gold chain that was rising and falling on her breast.

"Yes please." Maureen flushed with pleasure. All the gang would be there, and she'd be ever so proud of him. He didn't half look smashing in his uniform, too.

"Derek's got a present for you," said Mrs. Smith insinuatingly. " 'Aven't you, Derry?"

"Oh." Maureen looked coy. "You really shouldn't 'ave."

Derek was acutely uncomfortable at this deception. "I'll give it you tonight," he said, cleverly avoiding giving her the Greek necklace with all his family watching. "I got to unpack it."

Maureen stood up and smoothed her skirt, which was a tight straight one with provocative slits at the sides, and said, "Well, I'd better go and get ready. What time you callin' for me, Derry?"

"About eight," he said. "I'll meet you the corner of your buildin'."

He saw her to the front door, and just before he opened it he tilted her back against his father's coat which was hanging on the stand, and gave her a half kiss.

"Go on!" whispered Maureen, "your Mum might see us."

But whether or not it was an invitation, he opened the door and gave her a little push. She giggled, treated him to a last loving glance, and was gone with a slightly uneven tapping of the metal discs she had had nailed on to her high heels.

Derek hung about in the stuccoed entrance hall of the Palais, waiting for Maureen to emerge from the ladies' room. She came at last, and for a brief second the swinging door revealed to him that secret world of mirrors, plastic and chromium plate.

The fact that she had just left behind some private female aspect of her life made her extremely coy. She came towards him smiling, slipping her arm through his.

"I met Rose Limage in there." Her voice implied their quick whispered exchange of intimacies about him. "Do you think she's pretty, Derry?"

He squeezed her arm. "Not as pretty as you, Maur."

The words were almost lost in the sudden roll of drums. The next dance, said the M.C., who wore a maroon dinner jacket, would be a quickstep.

"Dance?" asked Derek.

She slipped into his arms and closed her eyes, fitting the curve of her head against his neck. The gelatine slides on the spotlight started turning, first green, then purple, then red. Over Maureen's head Derek watched the crooner twisting at the microphone. "I love you, I love you," he sang.

Maureen snuggled closer, and he moved his hand up from the small of her back to the soft nape of her neck. But it was a bit early in the evening to start that sort of thing. The dance ended and with linked arms they walked slowly off the floor towards the bar which said NO INTOXICANTS in red Gothic letters.

"What you want?" asked Derek.

"I'll 'ave a coke," she said, choosing delicately. "No I won't, I'll 'ave a raspberry fizz."

At the bar he met Rose Limage. He winked at her, and she winked back.

"We'll 'ave a dance later," he said in her ear, "if Maureen don't make too much fuss. Anyone buyin' you a drink?" She shook her head. "What you goin' to 'ave then?"

She chose a raspberry fizz too. The girl at the bar placed the glasses upside down over the tops of the bottles so that they looked like tooth-glasses on a wash-stand, and put them on a plastic tray scarred with brown cigarette burns. Derek led the way over to an empty table. Behind, boarded in gilded ply-wood, were the love seats, little alcoves for two where early in the evening you held hands, and later, if you were lucky enough to find one unoccupied, you kissed. Sometimes, he remembered, the M.C. would draw attention to some sheepish couple and the spotlight would single them out, blushing and entwined.

"Mind if I 'ave this dance with Rose?" he asked Maureen. "Won't be long." They stood up. "Be good while I'm gone."

Maureen sipped her raspberry fizz and tried to keep her eyes on them in the violet haze. But in a moment they were lost somewhere on the centre of the floor.

While they danced Rose didn't speak at all, and then suddenly she jerked away from him, and with mouth open wide and eyes narrowed to slits started an elaborate series of solo steps. She swung her hips and gave Derek what she considered a provocative look over her shoulder. Her whole performance was a minutely observed impersonation of a dance hostess in a second feature American film. It left him cold. He was glad when the dance was over.

At eleven he looked at his watch and said, "Let's go, Maur, shall we?" They were dancing very close, the music had changed its mood and the spotlight had been rose-pink for a long time. He felt her nod.

"Yes," she whispered. "I'll fetch my coat."

He followed her to the entrance way, and reclaimed his own rain-coat, bundled across the counter complete with little green ticket.

Maureen came out adjusting her headscarf. Neither of them spoke. Once outside in the street, with the lamps throwing refracted slivers of light along the wet surface of the road, he said, holding her arm tightly, "Where shall we go, Maur?"

She still clung to the romantic artificiality of the Palais. "What you mean, Derry?"

He was very conscious of the rain and his desire for her. He felt that the evening's dancing was sufficient preliminary, and he wasn't going to waste any more time courting her. He was walking quickly and she had to hurry to keep up with him.

He isn't half moody, she was thinking, not knowing whether to be thrilled or cross. Ever so passionate really.

"Come on," he said. "We can go down 'ere. They had stopped by a bomb-site two or three feet below the level of the road. The lamplight illuminated the first few yards, beyond that there was only shadow and the whitish outline of a wall. "Give us your 'and, Maur. I'll 'elp you down."

He swung himself down and took both her hands firmly. "Come on. Jump."

She practically fell. "My ankle," she said. "What you want to bring us down 'ere for I don't know."

He led her over the stones out of sight from the road, and put his arm round her waist. A tin can rolled from under his foot and rattled away into the night. "Give us a kiss, Maur," he said.

She started to resist him, and then responded. He leant her back against the wall and began to fumble with her blouse.

"Derry," she whispered. "You shouldn't."

But he went on kissing her, his hands still trying to force the buttons.

"Mind my clothes," she giggled. "They're gettin' all crumpled." She didn't know if she was enjoying it or not.

The noise of traffic passing in the street above them, together with oddly intrusive sounds, the bark of a dog and the hoot of a ship's siren far down the river like the contrived effects in a radio play, gave them a feeling of remoteness.

"Oh, Maur," he said, "I don't 'alf want you."

For a moment he almost loved her, the brilliantine scent of her hair, the hard pressure of her ear-ring against his cheek, and then, suddenly, it was cold and bleak and he felt tired. Maureen was breathing heavily in his arms, her scarf pushed at an untidy angle. He took his arms away. "Let's go," he said.

They made their way in silence back to the road. He grazed his hand badly on the rough stone, pulling himself on to the pavement, and hauled her after him.

"Derry?" Maureen hung on his arm. "Derry, I 'aven't never done that before. I 'aven't never let a man touch me before."

He wanted to shake himself free of her clinging arm. "Don't give us that," he said brutally. Not that he really cared. He was all at once terribly frustrated. This was what he'd been looking forward to. Evenings spent exploring the noisy bazaars of Istanbul, lazy afternoons when he had sprawled on deck watching the harbour-craft at Monte Carlo, had all projected themselves to this point when he would hold a girl in the familiar back streets of Mile End. His clothes were soaking with rain, his hand hurt him. He felt he ought to be talking lovingly to Maureen, or making love to her, and he couldn't do either. He sensed her disappointment and it only irritated him. They had reached her block of flats, and at the door he remembered the present. He made an effort to be nice to her.

"The present I brought you," he said.

"Oh, Derry." She unclasped the beads and put them on, trying to recapture a sentimental mood. "They're lovely." She put her arms round his neck to kiss him. "It's ever so nice 'avin' you back," she said softly, her breath hot against his mouth.

He kissed her quickly and disengaged himself. "Goodnight, Maur. I'll be pushin'. I've 'ad a day."

She had been all ready for more cuddling and fumbling in the dark doorway, but tried to understand his changing mood. "Goo'night, Derry." She hesitated, then said, "When'm I goin' to see you?"

"I don't know," he said. "I'll call round. I can't say when definite." He walked away hurriedly, putting up the collar of his raincoat, and turned into Jubilee Road.

II

The pigeons outside the window had been cooing and fluttering so loudly that Freda Mackenzie was awake when her alarm clock rang at half-past seven. Even so, it was a minute before her finger found the button to shut off the irritating buzz. Having silenced it she lay in bed and thought about the day. On Tuesday her teaching timetable left her two free periods and she was going out with Matthew in the evening. Also it was salad day for the L.C.C. and that was a school dinner she didn't mind eating. It saved her making sandwiches now and gave her more time to get dressed and prepare her breakfast. Freda disliked having to hurry, and preferred going without her breakfast rather than having to run to the station.

This morning she took her time, and gathered the scraps of breakfast toast to give to the pigeons. She lived at Bannerton Gardens, South Kensington, just off Gloucester Road, and her small converted flat looked out on to the gardens themselves. On warm days they were full of mothers and shouting children, even the occasional nanny, although nannies in South Kensington were becoming rather scarce.

Her flat was quite pleasant. She had a high bedsitting-room with a sloping ceiling, a small bathroom and an even smaller kitchenette. Her landlady had put flowered cretonne curtains at the dormer window, and allowed Freda to move the furniture, which was plain and good except for a cheap box-wood wardrobe. Freda had brought her own pictures, an expensive Utrillo print from Paris, and a Picasso reproduction carefully cut from a book of lithographs. She also had her own cushions and ornaments and, of course, her books. Really it was her room at college transplanted. She still gave Sunday afternoon teas with French bread and honey and cake to any of her college friends when they came to London.

By the time she was ready to leave it was twenty to nine. She picked up the pile of green exercise books, and went out, making sure the lock clicked behind her. On the way downstairs she met her landlady, Mrs. Gibson-Brown, who called out good-morning as she was taking in her milk and *Telegraph*.

Major Gibson-Brown had left his wife four years ago for a repertory actress in Brighton, and ever since, Mrs. Gibson-Brown had had to let part of her house to make ends meet. She had found it difficult to get the 'right' tenants, and was very happy to have Freda in her top flat instead of the model who had rented it before.

Out in the street the early May sun lit up the ponderously Italianate façades of the houses opposite, and shone on the plate-sized blue plaque which stated that a famous politician had lived in one of them. At each pillared porchway were rows of half-pint milk bottles, for these enormous houses, built originally for the middle classes of the nineteenth century, were now without exception converted into bed-sitting-rooms and maisonettes for the shop-girls and secretaries of the twentieth. At the tube station Freda had to run down the steps to catch her train before the doors closed, which made her breathless and annoyed.

The train was packed, and she stood leaning on the glass partition, while a small girl did her homework against the other side. Her neat uniform and velour hat indicated the sort of school she attended. Freda would have liked to have looked over her shoulder to see what work she was doing, in order to compare it with the standard in her own school. Since she had started teaching she felt proprietary about children. She couldn't see two small boys scuffling on a pavement without a strong desire to interfere. She often wondered if that was the way one eventually became a fussy school-marm. She looked at the other passengers and amused herself by trying to guess their private lives. It was easier to place those who got out at St. James's (insurance clerks and civil servants) than those who fought their way off at Charing Cross, or were obviously staying on till Barking.

It was the middle-aged working women who most interested her because they were what her own class of girls would become, sallow and tired, with bright cheap brooches pinned to threadbare coats.

At Mile End she found she was later than usual, and had to run to catch the trolley-bus. Two or three of her class were on it before her and called out "Mornin', Miss" down the gangway, and then dissolved into secret giggles which Freda felt must concern her. When she got off at Jubilee Road they joined her and carried her books into school. Boys and girls in the playground impeded her progress, and crowded round her telling her about the television programmes and the films they had seen the night before.

Later in the morning, seated at her desk in the classroom, with a pillar of bluebells wedged tightly in the jam-jar in front of her, Freda waited for the break-bell to ring. Usually she looked forward to the fifteen-minute respite, but today she was on playground duty which always made the morning seem long. Already her class had ears tuned for the clinking of bottles in the milk crates. Any moment she knew one of the girls would disturb the calm of the lesson. There were some days, and this was one of them, when the effort of exerting her personality over thirty-two others made her resort to bribery and offer a prize for the best handwriting. Prizes, she found, worked wonders.

Freda's class was the top class, and it was also the most difficult, for nearly a third of its members were on probation. This was her second term at Jubilee Road. Not long ago the local Education Office had decided the school should be renamed 'The Sunflower' but that was the only change made. No new equipment was ordered and the dingy Victorian Gothic classrooms remained over-crowded. "It's a happy school," the Divisional Officer told her when she got the job.

Since she had come down from University full of hopes that had been gradually dispelled, she had tried several jobs, none of which she had really liked. The last had been with an advertising agency, but the fat, successful little director had expected her to do 'extra-office' duties, which, she found, included 'cosy little suppers' together. So she had left and taken this job, a last measure, a stop-gap, as a Supply Teacher in a district which was glad of anyone, even without special training, to go from school to school wherever there was a temporary shortage of staff. Freda found the work interesting, although any ideas she may have had about helping the girls to develop wider interests were soon upset. Within a few weeks she realized that most of them would spend the rest of their lives raising families and working as 'chars'. The thing that had surprised her most of all, for it was an aspect of life quite new to her, was the high percentage of illiteracy, so that the brighter children seldom had a chance to do well. Their surnames seemed to be either exotic and foreign—Naposnic, Wassilevsky, Menetti—or blunt and almost as if they were not properly spelt— Iles, Prake, Britt—which was probably the case. A grandparent or a parent who only spelt phonetically, or perhaps never wrote their name down at all, would be responsible for that.

The girls wore new nylons every week and high heels when they could get away with it. They had disliked her predecessor Miss Thompson, and forced her to leave by organizing such chaos during her lessons that she found it impossible to teach. Miss Thompson had left in tears, miserable and bewildered. It had been her first post, and she had prepared her lessons with tremendous care, covered the walls with 'interesting' pictures, and arranged play-readings after school hours. Fortunately, the girls were kinder to Freda.

Now, waiting for the bell, with the sunlight splintering the glass of the goldfish tank in the window, and the noise of pen-nibs squeaking in the inkwells, she felt momentarily contented, in spite of the imminent playground duty.

"Miss?" It was Gladys Butler in the front row. "Miss, d'yer like dancin'?"

It had begun. The class was intent upon her answer. To a member she had their attention.

This was Freda's greatest failing as a teacher. She was defence-less against her class's insistence that their relationship should be a personal one.

"Yes, quite," she said.

"Do you go often, Miss?"

"No, not very often." She tried not to encourage such questions without making her answers seem starchy and unkind.

"I go, Miss, with my boy. 'E don't 'alf 'old you close, Miss."

"I'n't she awful? You got a boy, ain't you, Miss?"

There was quite an uproar.

"Silence!" cried Freda. "Get on with your work."

But it was too late.

"I can 'ear the milk comin'. Got the time, Miss?"

The bell, shaken vigorously by a specially selected small boy, began its rhythmic jangling in the main hall, passed along outside and died away down the corridor.

"Can we go?"

"When you are all quiet," said Freda.

"Shu' up, Mavis."

"Shu' up yerself."

"I won't. Oh, Miss, she's keepin' us all in. *Mavis.*"

"I'm waiting," said Freda coldly, her hands folded in front of her on the desk. 'I don't mind missing *my* break' her expression implied.

There was a momentary silence and she seized on it. "Out you go," she said.

With a great deal of pushing the girls clattered out into the corridor and down the stone steps to the playground. Gladys Butler lingered behind to offer Freda some unpleasant-looking toffees.

"Go on, Miss, 'ave lots. 'Old out yer 'an's."

"One's enough, thank you, Gladys."

But Gladys was disposed to be conversational. "I like yer 'air-cut, Miss." She stretched out an inky, nail-varnished hand to pat it.

This was one of the moments when Freda was at a loss. Her impulse was to slap the hand away, but that would make her look foolish. Besides, she had no doubt that Gladys would slap her back.

Miss Carstairs, headmistress over both the girls' and the boys' schools, appeared in the doorway.

"You're wanted on the telephone, Miss Mackenzie. I'll take over your duty until you can come down." She turned, a large and impressive figure, to Gladys. "I heard what you said, Gladys Butler. I have never heard anything so impertinent. I am most surprised. The first thing we learn here is that we are never personal to our teachers."

Middle-age and a dramatic bust did a lot for one's authority, thought Freda. Miss Carstairs lived with her mother and elderly sisters at Balham and was very keen on games.

"We are a good hockey school," she would say, announcing a result after prayers, as if this were Roedean. The girls had to go swimming once a week, winter as well as summer, unless they produced a genuine medical certificate.

"What nonsense," Miss Carstairs would cry, throwing into the wastepaper basket a letter laboriously written by one of the mothers.

"Off you go, Joyce! What you need is more exercise and then there'd be none of these stupid bouts of giddiness."

Freda was almost always in sympathy with the girls and they knew it. It gave them an advantage over her.

"Miss, you're too soft," Gladys Butler told her one afternoon when she was completely exhausted from trying to keep order. "We likes yer, but we can't 'elp playin' up."

The telephone was in Miss Carstairs's green-walled study. The religious calendar swung tapping against the wood of the door as Freda entered. The receiver lay in the wire letter basket. She picked it up.

"Hallo?" she said.

"Freda?" It was Matthew. "Look, darling, I'm sorry. I can't get away from the hospital until quite late, so we'd better call off this evening."

"What a bore," said Freda crossly. "That leaves me quite flat."

"Never mind," Matthew consoled. "I'll pick you up on Friday after school and I'll try to get tickets for something before that. Okay?"

"Lovely," said Freda.

"I must fly now, darling, sorry about tonight's mess-up."

Freda replaced the receiver and collected a cup of tea from the bare staff room. Then she went down to the playground where Miss Carstairs stood under the solitary plane tree which grew surprisingly from the waste of grey asphalt. She nodded to Freda and walked back into the school.

Freda was at once surrounded by a sycophantic group. One girl wanted to give out the milk, one to sit by her when she was next on dinner duty, one to carry her empty cup back to the staff room.

She felt a sudden rage at herself for not being able to keep them at arm's length and have five minutes in the playground alone.

Their conversation, which often instructed and entertained her, was today rather irksome. She was irritated that her evening had been left in the air, as she had been very much looking forward to seeing the new Italian film. She loved Italy and the realist style of the postwar Italian films. Besides she hadn't seen Matthew for two weeks.

The voices of the girls impinged on her thoughts.

"I saw your brother up the Palais larse night, Joan Smith," said Gladys Butler. " 'E in't 'alf 'an'some. You should see Joan Smith's brother, Miss," she went on, turning to Freda. " 'E's a sailor."

"Yeah, 'e went dancin' with our Maur," contributed Doris Lacey.

"I 'spect 'e's comin' up the school this afternoon," said Joan Smith, "to see Miss Carstairs."

"Fancy wantin' to see 'er," sniffed Gladys. Then, with a wink at the others, "She wouldn't know what to do wiv a sailor."

"That will do," said Freda. But she smiled inwardly at the vision of the impregnable Miss Carstairs indulging in a flirtation. All further speculations on the private life of the headmistress were cut short, however, by the ringing of the lesson bell.

Back in the classroom Freda set an arithmetic exercise for which she had an answer book. Maths were not her subject. Even School Certificate had been a struggle.

"I'm sorry," Miss Carstairs had said when, on her first day at Jubilee Road, Freda pointed out that it would be sensible if she did not take her class for arithmetic, "but our staff must be prepared to teach any subject." She had softened a little. "Don't let it worry you, Miss Mackenzie. It isn't at all advanced, and you will always find one girl who likes to show off and explain to the rest of the class."

So, for the time being, the arithmetic lessons in Freda's form were something of a farce, with Freda struggling to understand the text-book explanations, and frequently leaving it to the girls to work out a method for themselves.

As she sat compiling a tables test to give at the end of the morning, Freda suddenly became aware that Joan Smith was crying.

"What's the matter, Joan?" she asked in a gentle, reasonable voice.

The girls who could not see Joan without swivelling round on their chairs, swivelled.

"One of them teachers been on at you?" demanded Gladys. "Don't you take any notice of 'em, Joanie."

"I can't do me sums," Joan managed to say after a moment in which she made an effort to control her tears.

"Don't break your 'eart over any soddin' arithmetic," advised Gladys warmly. "She don't need to cry over that, do she, Miss?"

Freda told Joan to come out to her desk.

"Which sums are they, that are bothering you?" she asked.

"It's not any in particular, Miss. It's all sums." She leant heavily against Freda's chair. "I never been able to do 'em, not since I was at the Primary. Why've I got to keep on, Miss?" Her voice rose and ended in a sob. "I'm leavin' soon."

"That's right," said Gladys loudly. "She ought to be doin' sewin' when the rest of us is doin' our sums. No point in bungin' 'er 'ead up wiv figures when she wants to do tailorin'." She realized her unintentional joke and gave a peal of laughter, then continued her attack on Freda. "It's sense to me, Miss."

"It's sense to me, too," said Freda.

Gladys beamed and nudged the girl next to her.

"I'll speak to Miss Carstairs about it. There's really much more point in your having extra needlework practice. It's only for this term after all."

"Oh, Miss," Joan smiled blearily. "Do you think Miss Carstairs'll let me?"

"I don't know," said Freda, "but I promise I'll do my best to persuade her."

Acute misery during her own schooldays made her entirely sympathetic to Joan, but already she foresaw the objections Miss Carstairs would raise. The headmistress showed great understanding over social problems and home difficulties, but she was incredibly rigid when it came to individual variations in the school syllabus. She believed firmly in regimentation during the school day.

"It is the only training they have in their lives," she told Freda in an early interview with her. "It is good for them to do things they don't like sometimes. And it is our duty not to relax this principle."

Freda, who partly agreed with her, doubted whether she would relax the principle for Joan Smith.

By lunch time, the day which had begun so well appeared rather bleak. Lunch in the staff room was always a strain. The fact that today she ate a school lunch caused more comment than ever, for Freda's sandwiches never failed to raise eyebrows. She used continental bread and the fillings came from a delicatessen. Liverwurst and liptauer cheese remained a source of amusement to the rest of the staff, especially to Mr. Pethcart who preferred to tuck in to the grey shepherd's pie from the school kitchens.

Mr. Pethcart had been at Jubilee Road his entire teaching life. Nowadays he spent his lunch time arguing school politics with Miss Parrot, who was never without a copy of a left-wing weekly paper under her arm to support her views on corporal punishment or compulsory games.

Somehow, Freda usually became involved in these arguments, and tried desperately to arbitrate between the extreme factions.

"Discipline," Mr. Pethcart would say, "cannot be enforced without a bloody good whack with the stick."

Miss Parrot, who ate only yoghourt for lunch, would dip a teaspoon into the bottle and tell Mr. Pethcart with infinite patience that he really should make some attempt to be aware of modern methods.

"You've only got to look at Miss Mackenzie's class to see what modern methods do," said Mr. Pethcart nastily, "eh, Miss Mackenzie?"

Freda deliberately did not mention the question of Joan's arithmetic, knowing the exact form the argument would take. Sometimes she didn't know which she found more wearing, the staff or the girls.

During the first part of the afternoon she was free, and sat in an empty classroom reading a novel concealed in a more scholastic cover. For the last period of the day however, she took her class for the lesson called Current Events. She brought a paper with her, and read through and expounded briefly on the headlines. Then she asked for comments on any item of the week's news.

Gladys Butler put up her hand.

"Miss, that murderer up at 'Ammersmith. Will 'e be 'ung, Miss?"

It never varied. Sexual crimes were the most popular.

"Miss, why did 'e kill all them ladies?" she persisted.

"Because he was insane, Gladys."

"It was always ladies, wasn't it, Miss? 'E strangled 'em wiv their own stockin's. They found that young girl lyin' naked in 'er bed, the police did, didn't they, Miss? I think 'e ought ter be 'ung," she concluded, looking round for approbation.

"My Dad says no one didn't. They didn't, did they, Miss?" appealed Joan Smith.

"We discussed this last week," said Freda wearily. "Perhaps someone has something new to tell us. Doreen, how about you?"

Doreen, the highly strung product of a problem home, had a mouth full of chewing gum, which she occasionally blew out in a pink bubble between her teeth.

"Are you chewing again?" asked Freda in the way school teachers have when they know the answer.

"No," snapped Doreen, moving the gum to her cheek.

The class giggled.

"I think you are," said Freda, "and I've already spoken to you about it twice today. Please go outside."

A look of fear came over Doreen's face at the thought of being discovered in the corridor by Miss Carstairs. She planted her feet firmly on the floor.

"No," she said, her eyes down.

The lesson was completely forgotten.

"I've no intention of going on," said Freda, "until Doreen has done as she's told."

"I'm not goin'," said Doreen decisively.

"It would be a pity," said Freda, hoping to appeal to her Group

Loyalty, "to keep the whole class in to finish the lesson after school because you won't go out now."

"I don't care," said Doreen.

Freda stood up and walked between the desks until she was by the girl.

"Go along," she said firmly. She hated these situations when it became imperative for her to exercise her authority.

"No." Doreen's lip quivered. She suddenly pushed back her chair and ran to the door. "I 'ate this school," she shouted. "And you." Then slammed the door behind her.

"She's run 'ome, Miss," piped Joan Smith, who sat by the window, and spent most of the day looking out of it.

"I'm not interested any more," said Freda. "Miss Carstairs will deal with her tomorrow. We'll go on with the lesson before any more time's wasted."

"Please, Miss, I got a question," said Gladys Butler, triumphantly waving her hand in the air.

"Yes?" asked Freda.

"Please, Miss," asked Gladys Butler, "do you believe in 'angin', Miss?"

It had been a tiring day and Freda was upset by Doreen's behaviour. Sometimes, she felt, she was a thoroughly bad teacher, and although she told herself teaching was not her career, she minded about her lack of discipline. She cleared up quickly, locked her desk and went along to Miss Carstairs's study to discuss this matter, together with the problem of Joan Smith, with her.

Little groups of girls were sauntering in the corridor, putting on their coats, offering each other biscuits, eyeing the boys.

"Goin' up the station?" asked Gladys Butler, only too willing to walk with her. Gladys didn't wear a coat at all. She had on a skirt and a green and orange blouse belted on the outside. She was very plump and bouncing, not by any means unintelligent. Freda was really quite fond of her.

"No," she said. "I want to see Miss Carstairs first."

"About Doreen?" asked Gladys with cockney sharpness.

"About all sorts of things," said Freda.

She knocked at the study door. Miss Carstairs opened it.

"Come in, Miss Mackenzie," she said. "I'll be with you in a moment." She indicated the young sailor who was standing in front of her desk. "This is Joan Smith's brother, Derek, who has come back to see us."

Freda smiled at him.

"Joan is in my class," she said. "I'm glad to meet you."

III

By the time breakfast was over Derek was already bored. He could sit for hours on the mess-deck happily doing nothing, but here, at home, he quickly became restless. He was not used to planning his time. When Joan asked him to come up to the school the first afternoon, his reply had been that he didn't know what he'd be doing by then so he couldn't say.

It seemed a leave in itself waiting for opening time.

At eleven-thirty sharp he was in the William Tell drinking a pint and telling old Mr. Frost the publican where he'd been. By dinner time he'd have given two weeks of his leave to see Johnnie Cooper, or even Fauntleroy.

He and his mother had midday dinner by themselves. He liked being alone with her. In company he felt conscious of her stout-ness and the drab clothes she wore, and would have liked her to be slimmer and smarter. On their own her plainness didn't matter. For her part she found it difficult to question him about himself and his affairs now that he was grown up.

Once, soon after he had gone into the navy, he had come in very late and was rather drunk. Mrs. Smith, who had waited up for him, had ventured to ask where he'd been. "Up West," had been the laconic reply, and he had fallen asleep in the kitchen without another word. In the morning neither of them had referred to the episode. Now she contented herself by indulging him with his favourite meals, and asked only an occasional question about his work on board ship.

"You goin' up the school then?" she said, putting a plate of fried steak and onions in front of him.

"I expec' so," said Derek non-committally.

Secretly he was beginning to enjoy the idea of turning up there looking smart in his uniform. It would be fun, too, to meet Mr. Pethcart and Miss Carstairs on their own level. He remembered his envy of other old boys who were greeted cordially in the middle of a history lesson and shaken by the hand.

"Yeah, I'll go," he said after a moment, with pretended indifference. "I got to do somethin'."

He spent a whole hour smartening himself up. He heated the iron on the range to press his uniform. His mother watched him put a newspaper over the collar to save marking it, and thought sentimentally that the navy certainly taught the boys to look after themselves.

"You'll make a good 'ubby for someone one of these days," she said.

"Go on," said Derek, putting his weight on the iron handle, "you won't catch me gettin' spliced."

"What about Maureen?" asked his mother. "You like 'er, don't you?"

"Not that much I don't," he said. "What you think I'm goin' up the school for? I'm goin' to give Joan's class the once-over."

He decided to arrive at the school halfway through the last lesson, and so he set off at a quarter to four. It was quite nostalgic going up Jubilee Road and in through the playground gate again, walking over to the entrance with his shoes making that curious crisp noise on the asphalt.

He could hear the drone of Mr. Pethcart's voice inside the building, and a piano playing in the girls' school. From the open window came the sound of voices, rather off key, singing a sea-shanty. He caught the last words of the chorus:

"Wiv a comb and a glass in 'er 'and, 'er 'and, 'er 'and,
 Wiv a comb and a glass in 'er 'and."

With slight nervousness he knocked at Mr. Pethcart's door. The voice continued a moment, then called out "Come in!" and went on with an explanation of vulgar fractions.

Derek opened the door, and thirty pairs of admiring eyes immediately turned and examined him.

"Smith," said Mr. Pethcart, as if he'd seen him last week. "How's the navy?"

"Fine," said Derek, grinning. "Just back from the Med., Sir."

"That's grand," Mr. Pethcart nodded. "Very broadening for the mind. Smith used to be the worst boy in the class," he went on, turning to the boys. "And look at him now—defender of the Empire." Mr. Pethcart never minded if the class didn't understand his jokes.

"I don't know so much about defendin' the Empire," said Derek. "But I certainly 'ad a good time."

"Tell the class about your work," invited Mr. Pethcart. "If we stretch our imaginations, I think we can call it educational."

Derek enjoyed that. He stood by Mr. Pethcart's desk and glamorized his job to such an extent that one might have thought he was a ship's boy serving on a graceful old tea clipper, rather than an efficient piece of mechanism in a modern push-button navy. When he'd finished, and most of the class had made up their minds to go to sea, Mr. Pethcart said, "Thank you, Smith. Now, if you don't mind, I'll try and instil some arithmetical knowledge into these numskulls." He held out his hand and Derek took it. The interview was over. Sorry that he hadn't been able to prolong it, he went down to Miss Carstairs's study. He met her in the corridor.

"Derek Smith," she said. She never forgot a name. "How nice of you to visit us. Come and have a chat."

She preceded him into her little box-shaped room and sat down at the desk. The room hadn't changed one bit and neither had Miss Carstairs. She wore the same maroon costume and pale blue blouse he remembered, and the picture on the door was the same as before with a new calendar drawing-pinned to the bottom. He recalled standing on this very spot waiting for her to come and lecture him for brawling in the playground.

"Tell me," she was saying now, "what sports do you play in the navy? I expect you are in one of your ship's teams. Hockey was your game, wasn't it, Smith?"

"Yes," said Derek. "But I prefer soccer. And I row for the ship at naval regattas." He felt it a fraternal duty to ask after Joan's progress. " 'Ow's my sister doin'?"

"Very nicely," said Miss Carstairs, pleased at the enquiry, although family feelings were always strong in a school such as this. "Her needlework is extremely neat. I think we will be able to get her a good tailoring job when she leaves this year."

"Mum'd like that," Derek said. Tailoring was a local trade and an esteemed one—tailoring for girls and French-polishing for boys. Girls who did tailoring were always more classy than those in the factories, even if they didn't have quite such a good time.

He was finding the conversation a bit of a strain. He stood up, preparatory to making a few final remarks, when someone knocked at the door. He felt awkward, not knowing whether to go or stay, waiting hopefully for a sign from Miss Carstairs to indicate what he should do. It was a new teacher who came in. Derek realized with surprise that she wasn't much older than himself.

"This is Joan Smith's brother Derek, who has come back to see us," said Miss Carstairs. This new teacher smiled at him.

Derek was quite bowled over. She was really rather plain, he thought, if one compared her with Rose Limage for instance, but plain in a pretty way. He couldn't get nearer to it than that. She was quite small with a full mouth and an oval face, and she was a bit pale, yet—he looked her up and down—the rest of her wasn't so bad either.

"Joan is in my class," said the new teacher, holding out her hand. "I'm glad to meet you." She didn't wear nail-varnish although her nails were manicured, and she had an expensive-looking watch on her wrist.

Posh, thought Derek. He shook hands, and stood there feeling foolish.

"Pleased to meet you," he said. Then mumbled, "I'd better be goin'."

"What was it you wanted to see me about, Miss Mackenzie?" asked Miss Carstairs. "Will it take long?"

"Well yes," said Freda. "It will rather. There are two things. One, oddly enough," she looked at Derek, "concerns your sister. I think it would be quite helpful if Smith could stay," she went on, feeling she would need him as an ally. "Do you mind?"

"No." Miss Carstairs believed that co-operation between family and school was a sound foundation for proper treatment of the children. "I should be glad to hear his point of view."

"I'll try to 'elp," said Derek, immediately on the defensive in case Joan had got herself into a mess. "What's she been up to?"

"Nothing," said Freda. She smiled reassuringly. "It's just that she can't do her sums."

Derek looked relieved.

"Joan hates arithmetic," Freda continued, "and she is quite hopeless at it. Since she is leaving at the end of the term I wondered if it might not be more advisable if she did extra needlework instead."

"Yeah, she's goin' to do tailorin'," said Derek eagerly, warming even more towards Freda. He could have done with a teacher like her.

Miss Carstairs shook her head. "I'm afraid, Miss Mackenzie, that I can't possibly agree. If I let Joan Smith off her arithmetic, I should have half the school coming to me the next day asking to be let off goodness knows what."

Freda looked down at her hands for a moment.

"I don't want to argue with you, Miss Carstairs, but Joan is driven into such despair by her inability to do the work I set that she is often reduced to tears. Naturally I realize our aim here is to give the girls the best possible training for their future jobs, and I do feel that for Joan extra needlework would be of immense value. I understand one of the girls last year got a job in Hartnell's workrooms. It would be nice if Joan could have a similarly good start."

"Miss Mackenzie," said Miss Carstairs irritably, "from my point of view it would be a most unwise decision. Joan must do her arithmetic like everyone else in the school. I think the discipline will be of more use in her future life than two months' sewing lessons."

"Very well." Freda shrugged slightly. There was nothing she could add to alter Miss Carstairs's opinion. It would be foolish to make an issue of it. "The other thing I want to talk to you about concerns Doreen Robinson. She's being very difficult."

Miss Carstairs looked at her watch. "I'm afraid that will have to wait until tomorrow. I've got a board meeting at a quarter to five, and the governors are going to start turning up any moment now." She held out her hand to Derek. "Lots of luck, Smith. Don't forget to see us on your next leave. And tell your mother to come up at any time. I'm always happy to see her and discuss Joan's future."

"Good afternoon," said Derek. He grinned sympathetically at Freda. "Goodbye, Miss." He went out and closed the door behind him.

"A nice boy," said Miss Carstairs.

"Yes, he looks intelligent," said Freda.

Miss Carstairs nodded. "You're quite right. He was always a clean, tidy boy but the navy has made him seem more alert."

"I'll come and see you during the lunch hour tomorrow," suggested Freda.

"That will be best." Miss Carstairs took her maroon gloves out of a drawer and placed them on the desk, so that she could hurry home after the board meeting. She took her felt hat off a hook and put it beside the gloves. She always wore the same hat at exactly the same angle, and Freda could never understand why she still needed a mirror to put it on. Yet she spent at least three minutes every afternoon, and presumably every morning, arranging it.

"Goodnight, Miss Carstairs," said Freda. What shall I do this evening? she wondered as she hurried along the corridor. I think I'll go to the Italian film after all, Matthew or no Matthew, and suddenly she felt quite pleased at her independence.

She took her coat from the staff room, and put a pile of exercise books under her arm for appearances' sake, for she had no intention of doing any correcting this evening. On the oilcloth tacked to the table were eight thick white tea-cups and a plate of cakes made in the domestic science class. Gala treat for the governors, thought Freda.

She went down into the playground and across to the gate. It was very quiet now that the children had gone home. There was something eerie about the school when the children weren't there, as if one had just stepped aboard the *Marie Celeste*. Derek Smith was waiting outside the gate.

"Hallo," said Freda. "What are you doing here?"

"I wanted to ask you about 'ow Joan's gettin' on," said Derek. "You're 'er teacher. You know better than Miss Carstairs."

"She works very hard," Freda told him. "I like having her in the class. And I believe her cooking is good too." She smiled. "What more does a girl need?" She was finding it oddly difficult to talk naturally to this young sailor. She was used to dealing with old boys when they came back, but she was aware that what she was saying now sounded artificial and patronizing. It was due, possibly, to their meeting in Miss Carstairs's study. She had felt rather like a schoolgirl herself. Now she wanted to re-establish her position.

"Can I carry yer books?" asked Derek suddenly, holding out his hands for them. He practically took them.

"Don't bother," said Freda, "I can manage. This is where I catch my bus."

"I'm goin' down to Mile End myself," Derek insisted, "so I might just as well carry them, mightn't I?"

Freda laughed and handed them over. She looked at him, not quite able to make him out, yet amused by his persistence. It was quite natural in one way he should offer to carry her books. The children always did, and he was an old boy. He was also Joan's brother and his interest was pleasant and legitimate. Yet he wasn't merely offering to carry the books, he was asserting his right to do so. There was quite a difference. She was uncertain too, that before this moment he had had any intention of going to Mile End.

"Do you think Joan'll get a good job, Miss Mackenzie?" asked Derek, "even if she can't do sums?"

"She certainly should do," Freda said. "She really wants to do tailoring, doesn't she, Smith?"

"The name's Derek," he said, surprised at his own nerve. "I've left school now, Miss Mackenzie, you know."

It was a reproof. Freda glanced at him rather annoyed. But he looked so ingenuous standing there beside her, his white cap tilted on his forehead, and the pile of exercise books resting on the curve of his arm, it seemed impossible he was being impertinent.

On the bus he asked her which way she went home.

"Usually I go on the District line," said Freda, "but today I'm going to the West End to see a new Italian film."

"Italian?" asked Derek. "Do you speak Italian, Miss?" He sounded awed.

"Very little," answered Freda.

"What d'yer go for then, if you don't understand it?" He was mystified.

"There are subtitles," Freda explained. "The dialogue's written in English at the bottom."

"I never been to a foreign film," said Derek with interest.

"But you've been to foreign countries which is much better. You've been to Italy, haven't you?"

"Yeah, all over," he said. "Genoa, Naples, Pompeii." That was meant to impress. Being a school teacher she was bound to know all about Pompeii.

"Naples is fun, isn't it?" asked Freda.

He bought her ticket at the Underground, and one for himself as well.

"I thought you were only coming to Mile End," said Freda.

"No," Derek grinned. "I got nothin' to do. I'd just as soon ride down with you." He was suddenly daring. "You goin' to the flicks alone?"

"Yes," answered Freda, before she'd had time to check herself. "Yes I am." She could have bitten her tongue off.

Derek was silent for a moment, then he said, "Would you mind if I took you, Miss Mackenzie? I'd like to see a foreign film."

Freda all at once became more interested in him. Even if she wasn't very good at controlling her class, teaching was a thing that was deep in her. It would amuse and please her if she could awaken in him some response to a really intelligent film. She felt it was only necessary for someone to take the initiative and persuade him to go, and he would find he was able to enjoy a film he would have otherwise considered highbrow and difficult. She would enjoy watching his reactions. It was something of a challenge.

"Thank you, Derek," she said. "I'd like it very much. And it's about time you were weaned from Hollywood." She laughed.

"You talk like old Mr. Pethcart," he said. "It don't 'alf sound funny comin' from you."

"Why?" asked Freda foolishly. "Why funny from me?"

"You don't look like a teacher," said Derek. "Now do yer?"

She didn't answer. As a conversation she knew it would stay on one level. If she said "What does a teacher look like?" as she felt inclined, the answer was only too apparent.

They came out of the Underground at Baker Street and took a bus to Park Lane. It was a warm spring evening. Small groups were forming and re-forming round one or two orators at Speakers' Corner, and the park was fringed with flowers. People were sitting out in deck-chairs, and lying on the grass, and there were children's kites tugging at the sky.

"It don't seem believable," said Derek, "that it was rainin' cats and dogs yesterday, when we was paid off."

"Were," Freda corrected automatically. She blushed a little. "I'm sorry," she said. "It's habit."

Outside the Dorchester there was the usual array of expensive cars, and the ornamental jet of water dribbled unimpressively against the background of the hotel's curved façade. They walked along Curzon Street where a few prostitutes were already sauntering up and down. At the cinema Freda couldn't decide whether to offer to pay for herself. When he'd suggested taking her, she thought, he couldn't have been contemplating West End prices. But Derek, whatever his feelings, didn't appear dismayed.

The film was a good one. "I wish Matt were here," she thought at one point. But she checked herself. She was determined that Derek should not miss the subtleties of direction. "Do you see how the camera is angled," she whispered, "to give a feeling of insecurity?"

But only once did Derek speak to her. "That Adriana's a smasher, isn't she?" he said.

When it was over and they were out in the street again, he said, "I forgot they weren't speakin' English."

"It was good, wasn't it?" urged Freda. "You are glad you went?"

"I enjoyed it," said Derek. He looked down at his feet a minute, and then up at the dark evening sky. "I can't take you to 'ave somethin' to eat, Miss Mackenzie. If I'd 'ave known I'd 'ave brought more money with me."

Shall I ask him back for a meal? thought Freda. No, she decided, I won't. It's much better to leave it like this.

"I'll see you 'ome," he offered. Perhaps he had the same idea.

"Oh no, you mustn't do that," said Freda. "You've got a long way to go, and so have I, and we live in opposite directions. But thank you very much." She held out her hand. "It's been great fun. Goodnight, Derek."

He took it. "Goodnight. Thanks a lot for lettin' me go with you."

She was rather relieved not to have to go out for a meal somewhere, and have to force conversation. She wanted her own flat and solitude. "Goodnight," she said again, taking the exercise books from him. He watched her walk away up Curzon Street. What a lark, he thought, taking a school teacher to the pictures. Joan wouldn't believe him. Then he decided not to tell her. It would be unfair on Miss Mackenzie, the girls wouldn't half tease her. He heard a clock strike nine. There was no need to go home yet. He turned down towards Piccadilly instead.

Derek usually ended up at the Red Shield after an evening in the West End. As always it was packed full and very smoky. He edged his way to the bar and ordered himself a pint.

A voice behind him said, "Buying your own drinks, Jack?"

He looked round and saw a Piccadilly tart, and not a bad looker, either. She had blondish hair tied into a horse's tail with a piece of black ribbon, and a jacket of a very bright yellow with brass buttons.

He shifted from one elbow to the other and handed her a cigarette. She flicked a little black lighter and Derek held her wrist to steady her hand. He looked at the lighter which had on it her initials in imitation marcasite.

"What's the R stand for?" he asked.

"Rita," she said.

"Want a drink?"

"Thanks." Rita put her large patent-leather handbag on the bar and smiled at him. "On leave, Jack?"

"Yeah." He nodded. "Just back from foreign."

Rita looked knowing. "Bored already, I bet."

"Up till now," said Derek slyly.

She moved a little closer. "Coming back with me?"

Derek shook his head. "Sorry, Rita, I 'aven't got much on me tonight."

She was not offended by his business-like attitude. "That's all right, Jack. It's my night off. How about it?"

I suppose I might as well, he thought. I can't turn down an offer like this. He was never quite sure just how much he enjoyed having this sort of 'good time'. But it gave one status on the mess-deck. Already in his mind he was embellishing the incident for the benefit of his messmates.

"Thanks," he said. "I guess it's my lucky night."

"Let's go, shall we?" suggested Rita. "I got a place in Rudolph Street."

"You 'aven't 'ad that drink," he pointed out.

"There's plenty back home," Rita said. "No need to waste the money you have got."

He followed her out into Piccadilly. They pushed through the groups of drifting people, moving obliquely, like mosquitoes over a pond. News-stands, which during the day had sold all the usual magazines, now displayed thin paper books with lurid covers deco-rated by what seemed like the voluptuous prototypes of the girls walking along Coventry Street. There were also sealed envelopes with insinuating titles about flagellation and corporal punishment. Derek had once bought one, but all the envelope contained was a booklet telling the story in early English, of an obscure mediaeval martyr. He considered it a very disappointing waste of seven and sixpence.

"Down here, Jack," directed Rita, her gilt hair flopping against the collar of her jacket.

In Rudolph Street she unlocked a door and took him up several flights of stairs to her flat. A tray of drinks stood on a glass-topped table. There were satin cushions and net curtains and lamps shaded with rose-pink plastic.

"Nice, isn't it?" said Rita. "I can relax here. Sit down, Jack. Make yourself at home." She slung her jacket on to the divan. "Help yourself to a drink."

He heard a movement in the next room. "Who's in there?" he asked.

"That's all right, Jack," said Rita. "It's only my boy friend." She went to the door and opened it. "Come in, Bert, and meet our guest."

Bert wore a wide-shouldered gaberdine suit of light blue, and a red satin tie with a metal bird on it. His hair was brushed back elaborately and he grew a little moustache. On his hand there were two heavy rings, one of which had a large red stone.

"Always pleased to meet the navy," said Bert cordially. He poured himself a drink, and one for Derek as well. Then he switched on the radiogram and started to sort out records.

"We must all get to know each other, mustn't we?" said Rita, putting her hand on Derek's shoulder. "Make yourself real comfy, Jack. Take off your jumper."

I don't get this, Derek thought to himself. What the hell does she want me for with that creep around?

Rita perched on the arm of his chair. "I bet you're making Bert quite jealous," she said. "A handsome boy like you. What we going to do about it?"

"It's not my bloody fault if he's jealous, is it?" said Derek with asperity. "You brought me 'ere."

"All right, all right," Bert soothed him. "Rita didn't mean to upset you. She only wants us all to get on well together, don't you, Rita?"

"That's right." She leaned back. "Three's company, I always say."

"Come on, Jack," said Bert. He began to undo his tie. "Why don't you take some of them clothes off?"

It suddenly dawned on Derek what was expected of him. He could have kicked himself for being so slow. He pulled himself out of the chair. "I'm sorry," he said curtly, "but three's not my line." He picked up his cap and put his half-empty glass back on the tray.

"Don't be like that," said Rita. "We can all have a good time together."

He was already at the door.

"You navy blokes are always scared," called Bert.

Derek didn't bother to look round, but slammed the door behind him. He felt slightly sick and it was a relief to be out in the street again. Johnnie would never believe him. I must be crazy, he thought, walking out on a bit of crumpet like that. Some leave this was turning out to be. All he'd thought about for ten months was women, and then when he had it handed to him on a plate, he turned it down as if he was the Pope.

It wasn't only this piece of goods, either. Maureen had been mad for him to go on pawing her for hours last night, and he'd let her go. I don't know what's good for me, he said to himself severely as he hurried along towards the underground. That's what's wrong with *me*.

IV

It was the last period of the afternoon, and Freda glanced up in the middle of a rather successful lesson she was giving on the French Revolution, while an illustration of a guillotine was passing from desk to desk. Through the open window she saw Derek Smith crossing the playground. Joan Smith, who had obviously not been concentrating, gave a little cry of pleasure.

"Miss, there's my brother!"

Several of the girls stood up, and the rest craned their necks in an effort to see him.

"I'm goin' down," said Gladys, "to do me Rita 'Ayworth act."

"You try," advised Doris Lacey, "and I'll smash yer face in. 'E's my Maur's."

Doris Lacey, whom Freda had always considered dull and uninteresting, all at once became the focus of her attention. Was this the sort of girl, she asked herself, that Derek took out on his leaves? Was her sister Maureen dim and mouse-like too? She vaguely recalled meeting Maureen at the Christmas party, but couldn't remember if she was the one who giggled all through her dance with Mr. Pethcart, or the one wearing black lace who leant up against the piano looking sullen until it was time to go home. But she had never seen Doris display any temper before.

"Can I go down, Miss?" shrieked Gladys.

"I warn yer!" said Doris ominously.

"No, of course you can't," said Freda. "The bell hasn't rung."

"I want to go to the offices, thank you very much." She said this in a self-satisfied, ultimatum-giving voice.

"You must wait," Freda said patiently.

Gladys turned to the class.

"Our doctor says you can die if you don't go when you want. My Mum'll be comin' to see yer, Miss Mackenzie," she threatened, "if you don't let me go to the lavvy when I want."

The class laughed appreciatively.

"She don't want ter go," said Doris knowingly. "She only wants to go down and see Derek Smith."

"I'm quite aware of that," Freda answered.

The bell rang. Gladys Butler was busy putting on lipstick behind the lid of her desk, and making eyes at Freda over the top of it.

"It's not lipstick I'm puttin' on, Miss. It's stuff to stop my lips gettin' all chapped." She tittered. "The doctor give it me."

Freda had soon discovered that the doctor's advice and prescriptions were a common excuse for breaking school rules. Sweets, for instance, were always cough sweets prescribed by the doctor for a bad throat.

I can't be bothered to argue today, she thought. She pretended she hadn't heard, and went on locking her desk and the cupboards. She could never believe it was necessary to lock up everything like this. Individually the girls seemed honest. But Mr. Pethcart had assured her rules of that kind weren't made for fun.

"Quite the wrong approach to the undeveloped mind," asserted Miss Parrot. She had deliberately left her desk drawer unlocked for several weeks, and then suddenly started locking it again.

"Missing something?" Mr. Pethcart had enquired, seeing her turn the key one afternoon. Miss Parrot blushed.

"Certainly not," she had snapped.

Mr. Pethcart was still enjoying the joke a term later.

In the staff room Freda repaired her own make-up with extra

care. I'll give the girls time to go home, she thought, before I go down.

As she descended the tiled-walled stairway to the playground, she was aware she hadn't lingered long enough. By the door, Derek was the centre of a giggling group.

"Come along, Gladys," said Freda rather unkindly, but to cover up her own slight discomfiture. "You must do your Rita Hayworth act outside the playground."

"You're jealous, Miss," someone said. "I'n't 'e lovely?"

Derek suddenly detached himself from them.

"Can I carry yer books, Miss?" he said, looking Freda straight in the eye, and fell into step beside her.

"Wha' er cheek," said Gladys furiously. "Stoppin' me, and then slinkin' off wiv 'im 'erself. Don't think I 'aven't seen yer, Miss," she called.

"You could 'ardly think that, could you?" said Derek.

"I'll never live this down," sighed Freda. "You've ruined me."

"Not yet I 'aven't," said Derek quickly. He had answered without thinking, the way one did with girls. There was a silence.

"I'm sorry, Miss Mackenzie," he said. "I didn't mean that."

"That's all right," said Freda coldly. She was conscious she had encouraged him to mild flirtatiousness, and yet when he responded, she was angry.

They had reached the bus-stop.

"Don't be mad at me," said Derek, "or you won't say yes to what I come for."

"What was that?" asked Freda, half-guessing.

"I wanted to give yer the meal we couldn't 'ave last night. Can I?"

Freda thought for a moment. She was aware how foolish it would be to accept.

"That would be very nice," she said.

"Where'll we go?" asked Derek eagerly. "You know the sort of places. I don't."

"I've got some things to do first, Derek," she said. "I'll meet you again at about half-past seven."

He looked slightly disappointed.

"Okay. Tell me where."

"Oh, somewhere central. The Underground at Oxford Circus? The ticket office?" Her voice was still slightly unfriendly.

"Righteo. Oxford Circus, seven-thirty. See you then, *Miss*." He emphasized the word. He wasn't going to let her get away with that high and mighty lark. Either she came out with him, or she didn't, but he wasn't going to go on accepting this teacher-old-boy relationship.

There was slight constraint between them. Then as her bus drew up, Derek gave a half salute of farewell.

"S'long, Miss Mackenzie," he said.

Freda climbed the stairs to her flat, and Mrs. Gibson-Brown came out on to the first landing to greet her.

"Your young man's been on the telephone, Miss Mackenzie. He wants you to ring him straight away." The only telephone in the house was in Mrs. Gibson-Brown's sitting room. The *salon*, she called it. It was a large over-furnished room, filled with family photographs and relics of a former middle-class gentility. A large cabinet was crammed with oddments of silverware—an enormous tea-pot, a cruet with tessellated turrets made to look like a castle, ivory and ebony fans, and a black leather box kept open to reveal a row of heavy Victorian dessert spoons lying on a padded bed of faded blue satin. Mrs. Gibson-Brown referred to this collection as 'the family silver'. Surprisingly, a leather-framed photograph of Major Gibson-Brown still stood on the grand piano. Freda had never heard the piano played, but it was always kept open, with a book of Schubert's songs on the music rest.

Freda followed her into the room, and said, "I'll 'phone now, then, if you don't mind."

She put three pennies into the money-box beside the telephone—the money-box was a cottage with a slot in the thatched roof—and dialled the number of the hospital. She was always shocked at the length of time they took to answer.

"I might be dying," she said to Mrs. Gibson-Brown. Mrs. Gibson-Brown knew all about Matthew, and where he worked.

The grumpy voice of the hospital porter answered her at last.

"I want to speak to one of the students, please," said Freda. "Mr. Matthew Taylor. It's important."

She was switched through to the canteen, then Matthew himself came to the telephone.

"I'm free tonight," he told her. "What about it?"

"I'm sorry, I can't," Freda said, realizing that this was the first time she had ever let him down. "I'm going out."

"Can't you put it off?" He sounded hurt.

For a minute she contemplated not turning up for Derek. He probably won't even come himself, she thought, remembering the inflection of his voice when they had parted. And Matthew of course was more important than Derek Smith. But it wouldn't hurt Matthew for once, to see that she could be busy too.

"It's really not possible," she said.

"Very well, I'll see you on Friday." He rang off, annoyed.

Mrs. Gibson-Brown, who had been patting up Regency-striped cushions on the ottoman, obviously couldn't decide whether or not to admit to listening. She permitted herself to have heard the last sentence or two.

"It always encourages them, dear," she said, "if they think they aren't the only pebble on the beach."

Freda found Mrs. Gibson-Brown's rather Victorian implications on how and how not to conduct a romance extremely irritating.

"It's the first time I've ever had to do it," she said abruptly. "And it happens to be genuine."

"I'm just going to make a cup of tea," offered Mrs. Gibson-Brown. "Won't you join me?"

"I'm afraid I haven't time," apologized Freda. "I must do some work, and I want a bath before I change. Thank you all the same."

Regretfully Mrs. Gibson-Brown saw her to the door. "Another time," she said.

In her own flat Freda was suddenly faced with the problem of what to change into. If she looked too smart Derek would be embarrassed, but on the other hand, she wanted to be attractive so that he would be pleased to be seen with her. She knew what the East End girls wore when they went out with their boys. If she didn't dress up, he might think she hadn't bothered.

She put on a woollen frock that she hoped was a compromise, and found herself dressing with greater care than she did for Matthew. Derek, she felt, would be even more critical.

As she left to meet him she again had the feeling that he wouldn't be there. She had known one or two young men who had behaved in that cavalier fashion. But Derek was there before her. He had been home and blancoed his cap for the second time that day. He looked young and fresh, and pleased to see her. He guided her by the elbow up the stairs to the street.

"Well?" he demanded. "'Ave you decided where we're goin'?"

"Oh dear," said Freda. "I'd forgotten all about it."

She went over the Soho restaurants in her mind. He obviously wanted it to be somewhere different, not the kind of place he usually went to. But she hadn't the faintest idea of a sailor's pay, and experienced the same feeling of embarrassment she'd had over the cinema tickets the night before. There was another factor, too. She didn't want to bump into anyone she knew. Which is what makes this sort of thing quite impossible, she told herself. I won't go out with him any more.

"Well?" asked Derek again.

"I know quite a pleasant little place," she said, thinking of one off Dean Street, reasonable, not smart, but where the food was excellent. Derek wouldn't be uncomfortable, and neither would she. She was pleased at having thought of it.

They turned from Oxford Street into Soho, that curious world of enormous cinema offices, continental food shops and mysterious little doorways.

"I don't know this part very well," said Derek, "tho' I come to a club around 'ere once with a bloke."

"What sort of club?" asked Freda.

"Oh, you know. One of them places where you can get drinks after eleven, full of women and men in duffle coats. I didn't go for it much," he added, "'cept for the drinks we 'ad."

"It does sound rather dreary," said Freda. "Here we are."

He pushed open the door and stood back for her to enter. She had often been here with Matthew, and the large Frenchwoman who ran the place knew her well. There were two floors, and Freda preferred it upstairs, because there each table was lit by an individual lamp, which made it seem both gayer and more intimate than the hard strip-lighting downstairs.

The speciality of the restaurant was *escalope de veau*, cooked with garlic, and Freda told Derek this before they got there, to avoid difficulty with the menu. She didn't call it *escalope*. Fried veal, she said. But it occurred to her that Derek would have eaten foreign food before.

When the meal was served, she asked him what he had eaten in France.

"Steak and chips," was the reply. "Better than you get 'ome 'ere."

"But didn't you try any of the local dishes?" she asked.

"No. Just steak and chips."

"Why?" She was thoroughly puzzled.

"I dunno," he said. "I suppose it's because I might not like them strange dishes when I'd ordered 'em, and food's expensive abroad, and it would be a waste of money, wouldn't it? Besides," he added, "I can't read French menus, but they always 'ave beef-steak written down, like in English."

"What a pity," Freda said. "I don't think there's much chance of your not liking what you ordered, they're such good cooks in France. You must try next time."

He smiled at her school-teaching voice. "Perhaps I will." Then, more to the point, "What you goin' to 'ave to drink?"

She ordered a glass of wine, and he asked for a pint of black and tan, and had to explain to the waiter what it was. They sent out for the drinks.

Freda felt surprisingly at ease with him, now that they were settled at the table without mishap, and curious about his background.

"What are you going to do when you come out of the navy?" she asked. "Or are you in for always?"

"I'm signed on for seven years," he said. "I got three more to go."

"And then what?"

"I dunno," he said lazily. "Somethin'll turn up, I suppose. Might even sign on again."

Freda had heard this attitude from her class a hundred times, and was always trying to fight against it. In Derek, however, it seemed rather charming.

"Won't it make you restless?" she pursued, "having travelled so much?"

"No," said Derek. "I like travellin', mind, but one bar ain't so very different from another."

Was he serious? Freda couldn't decide.

"Is that all you do, when you go ashore? Go to bars?"

"Yeah. That an' the brothels." He was quite unconcerned. "I remember once we was in Spain, Barcelona, the last port of call, and we couldn't find one nowhere. We'd just got back on board, when a bloke tells us about one along the road. So off we goes again, tells the ratin' on watch we'd only be gone five minutes."

He laughed reminiscently. Freda was still uncertain whether or not it was a line, a man-of-the-world pose, in order to impress her.

"So we rushes off, and there we was, in front of a ruddy great door, like a stable. And we banged and shouted, and no one came. We was just about to go back, when a little old man come round the corner, with a key as big as that plate, and in we goes.

"We crossed a courtyard place, and went into the 'ouse. Right in front of us was a door, with 'Lolita' written over it. But one of the blokes didn't like the name, so we went upstairs. On the first floor was another door, what said 'Pepita's'. We was just goin' in there, when we meets two of the lads comin' down. 'Conchita's is smashin',' they said. So we went on up to Conchita's. We banged on 'er door, and she come out in a yellow evening dress lookin' like . . ."

He broke off sheepishly. "I'm sorry," he said. "I oughtn't to be tellin' you all this."

But Freda was laughing.

"You've been to all the most sophisticated places in Europe," she said, "but all they mean to you is brothels and bars."

"Yeah," he agreed, not in the least offended. "That's 'ow it is in the Andrew."

"The Andrew?" she asked.

"That's what we call the navy."

"Why?"

"Well, back in the times when they used to 'ave press-gangs, there was a press man called Andrew Miller. 'E forced so many blokes to join, that it got known as Andrew's navy. Then they shortened it to the Andrew. See?"

He was obviously enjoying himself telling her all these things and he sensed her absorption in what he was saying.

Freda realized suddenly that it was not difficult to make conversation as she had expected, and what was more, she found herself really interested in his stories.

"What made you take up teachin', Miss Mackenzie?" he asked, thinking perhaps he'd talked too much.

Freda put down her wine-glass.

"My name's Freda," she said.

"Thanks, Freda." He took it quite naturally. "I was wonderin' when you was goin' to say that. I didn't like to ask. I never met a Freda before."

She began to tell him about herself, the jobs she'd taken, and why, now, she was teaching at Jubilee Road.

Derek interrupted her.

"I think the bloke over there knows you," he said. " 'E keeps on starin'."

"Where?" said Freda. After a moment she casually looked round. It was Matthew. Although he had first brought her to the restaurant and they had often eaten here together, she had taken it for granted he would go back to his digs tonight, since he was not with her.

She felt herself blushing.

"I do know him," she said to Derek. "He's a medical student, an old friend. As a matter of fact," she said with sudden confidence, "he asked me out tonight, and I turned him down." She could never become used to the way you bumped into people in a place as large as London. Yet you did. Time and time again, in the street, in a restaurant, at the cinema.

They had finished their meal now, and the waiter brought the bill.

"It's cheaper than I thought," said Derek.

Freda tried to see if he was leaving a tip, but she couldn't read the bill properly upside down.

They passed Matthew's table on the way out. It was a ridiculous situation. She knew him so well, they had been friends so long, but they were behaving like strangers.

"Surprise, surprise," he murmured, as she went past.

Freda stopped to speak to him. "I'm sorry about tonight," she said, hoping Derek was well out of earshot. "I couldn't get out of it."

Derek had walked ahead of her, and was waiting at the street door. It was only nine o'clock.

"What now?" he asked. He obviously didn't want to finish the evening so soon.

"I don't know," said Freda. "It's too late for a film. What would you do if you weren't with me?"

"Go to a pub," he said.

"Can't I go with you?"

"No." He shook his head. "I wouldn't take you to the pubs I go to." He was very firm.

"Let's walk then?"

He took her arm. "Okay, Freda. Which way?"

They crossed through Piccadilly, and into Green Park. It was a warm evening, but dew was beginning to rise. Attendants were busy closing up damp green deck-chairs, and piling them under the trees. Freda and Derek didn't hurry. It took them three-quarters of an hour.

"You live near 'ere?" asked Derek.

"Quite near," Freda said. "In Kensington."

"With your Mum and Dad?"

"No, on my own. I've a small flat. My parents live in the country, and I go home at weekends."

"Do you want me to see you back?"

"No," Freda said. If she asked him to do that, she would have to ask him in for coffee too, and she wasn't keen on the idea. Mrs. Gibson-Brown would certainly comment if she saw a sailor going up her stairs at half-past ten at night. "No thank you, Derek. It's so out of your way."

He didn't press the point. They were under the bus shelter now. He faced her urgently.

"When can I see you again? Tomorrow?"

"Tomorrow I must do some correcting," she said.

"Friday then?"

"On Friday I'm going out."

Derek was quick on the mark.

"With the bloke we saw in the restaurant?"

Freda nodded. "Yes, that's right."

"When can I see you, then? Or don't you want to come out again?"

"'Phone me round about Tuesday," Freda suggested. "We can fix something up then."

He wrote her number down on the carton of his cigarette packet. Her bus swung round the corner by St. George's Hospital. He was suddenly anxious.

"You aren't goin' to make excuses when I ring, are you?"

"No," said Freda. "I'm not going to do that." But she had given herself a loophole. She stood on the platform of the bus. "Goodnight, Derek. Thank you."

"Goodnight, Freda. Be seein' you."

She felt curiously happy as she opened her purse for the fare.

V

"Miss, your friend's waitin' for you." One of the smaller girls put her head round the staff room door, knocking inaudibly as she spoke. Behind her two or three of her friends were pushing her forward and whispering.

"'Ow's Derek Smiff?" she gasped suddenly. Laughter and a stifled shriek from the corridor greeted this daring question.

Freda was sitting at the table, adding the weekly marks.

"I don't know," she said. "You'd better ask Doris Lacey."

"We saw yer go off wiv 'im, Miss," said the girl, encouraged by her success.

"Perhaps you didn't see me leave him at the bus-stop?" suggested

Freda equably. "Did you say someone wanted me?"

"Yes. Your boy, Miss. 'E's outside in 'is car."

Freda's father had met her after school on one occasion, and when she had entered the classroom the next morning she had been greeted with cries of " 'Oo's got a sugar-daddy?" and " 'E's a bit old for yer, Miss, ain't 'e?"

But Matthew was a fairly familiar figure, and no longer caused excitement when he arrived in his vintage sports car. He was simply "Miss's boy".

Freda went out and climbed in beside him. He leaned across and closed the door.

"Who was the sailor?" he asked, as they drove off.

Freda flushed slightly. "Oh, a kid from school."

"Rather an old kid, isn't he?" Matthew asked. "What's the line, sweetie?"

"Don't be silly," said Freda crossly. "There isn't a line. He came up to the school, that's all. His sister's in my class and we got talking. He was anxious to see a foreign film and asked if I would go with him. He couldn't afford a meal afterwards, so he asked me to eat with him the next day, and I thought it rather sweet and amusing. I hadn't the heart to turn him down. Besides," she added, "I didn't expect to see *you* till today."

Matthew turned his head and smiled at her. They drove in silence for a while, then, as they waited at the traffic lights, he said, "Guess what the tickets are for?"

"I don't know," said Freda, still annoyed. "How can I possibly guess when there are at least thirty theatres in the West End?"

He pretended not to notice her continued irritation. "I'll tell you then." He named a witty play, translated from the French, that had been well received by the critics. *Elegant, Deliciously Naughty, I Have Never Been so Enchanted*, said the posters outside the theatre. Freda had been longing to see it for weeks.

"Oh, Matthew," she said, "you are an angel."

"We'll have an early meal," he suggested. "I'm not mad about a late night."

"No, nor me," said Freda. "Where shall we go?"

They drove into the West End and, since they were so early,

looked in at one or two of the Bond Street galleries. Then they walked through Mayfair to a smart little oyster bar, and eventually on to the theatre.

The play was trivial but cleverly acted, and the costumes and décor amusingly fantastic, but somewhere in the middle act Freda was overcome by a feeling of intense boredom. What was the play saying? What was the point? She had heard it, seen it, read it all before. It was sophisticated, decadent and quite unimportant. Why had she wanted to see it? One went around saying "I must see such and such a play," or "I simply have to go to such and such a film." Sitting there in the dark auditorium her pursuit of culture seemed suddenly irrelevant and pointless. Certainly theatre- and concert-going could be stimulating, uplifting even, but was it not, in the end, only one degree removed from the more physical, sensual pleasures of life—eating, drinking, making love— merely a more elaborate and subtle way of enjoying oneself? Or did a knowledge of the arts indirectly refine one's taste and develop one's understanding of human problems? Derek, for instance.

Was it right for her to attempt to interest Derek in good films, and good food, to try and introduce him to all the trimmings of a higher standard of living? Was it kind to wrench the boy from his social plane, so that he would be discontented with the views and ideas and tastes of his family and surroundings? Theoretically, thought Freda, it could only be right. At least, when it took place on the stage and in sociological textbooks, but in practice she wasn't so sure. The simple straightforward pattern of Derek's life was perhaps not only right for him, but necessary as part of the structure of society.

She realized suddenly that the curtain was descending. She had not listened to the dialogue for at least five minutes. The houselights came up, and she joined in the applause.

In the crowded bar, half-listening to the conversations round her, she was amused at her reflections on art and society, and her rather muddled attempt at analysing her relationship with Derek. Hardly a relationship, she thought. I've only met him twice.

After the theatre she and Matthew drove back to Bannerton

Gardens. He switched off the engine and quietness descended again on the street.

"Coffee?" she asked him.

"Please." He helped her out of the car.

As they climbed the stairs, Mrs. Gibson-Brown managed to coincide with them outside her door.

"Just locking up, Miss Mackenzie," she said. She smiled ingratiatingly at Matthew. Medicine was such a noble profession for a young man. "Good-evening, Mr. Taylor."

She felt it her duty to try and impose a rule of no guests after ten. She let flats to single girls only, and their mothers usually preferred it. "But I don't mind in the least your inviting Mr. Taylor up in the evenings," she told Freda. "He's so trustworthy."

"Good-evening, Mrs. Gibson-Brown," answered Matthew. He murmured something else in Freda's ear, which she hoped Mrs. Gibson-Brown hadn't heard.

Up in her flat she put some coffee to percolate on the stove.

"Anything to eat?" she asked.

He stretched out his hand from the armchair where he was sitting. "You," he said. He pulled her down on to his lap, and kissed her ear.

"Oh, Matthew." Freda got to her feet. "I'm doing the coffee. I can't be made love to now."

"I'll make love to you exactly when I want." He stood up, caught her back from on her way to the kitchen, and kissed her. "You try and stop me!" He meant it as a joke. He was playing caveman.

But Freda was irritated. She pulled herself free impatiently. "I've no intention of struggling," she said, "but the coffee will be boiling over." She moved to the stove and lifted the percolator from the gas, while he watched, amused, from the doorway of the kitchenette. She arranged the cups on a tray with deliberate slowness and carried them into the sitting-room. He stood aside to let her pass, and as she put the tray down on the low table, he came up behind her and put his arms round her waist.

"Please, Matthew," she said, surprised at the frigid tone of her voice. "We may have just seen a French farce, but do we have to act as if we're in one ourselves?"

"I've never noticed it bothering you before," said Matthew, "but if you prefer Greek tragedy, I'll pull an appropriately long face." He sat down in the armchair again. "Only I don't want to be late home tonight."

She was suddenly furious at the implication.

"I'm sick to death of being taken for granted," she said. "Simply because we've been out together, you assume we come back here to make love."

"Oh, come off it!" said Matthew. "Don't be so stupid."

"I mean it," said Freda. "Cream?"

"Please." It put him out to have to answer civilly. "For heaven's sake, Freda, why the middle-class morality? Or is it supposed to whet my appetite?"

"I'm sorry," said Freda. "I'm just tired of the routine acceptance of ending our evenings this way."

"I'll leave you to your virgin sheets then," he said, standing up. "When the mood passes let me know, and we'll make a date. Unless you're going out with your sailor boy-friend?"

He walked angrily to the door. Then suddenly his anger disappeared. He blew her a kiss.

"Sorry, sweetie. It took me by surprise, that's all." He came back into the room, and kissed her affectionately. "I'll ring you soon."

Freda felt sorry for having been so cross, but he let go of her hands and went again to the door.

"Goodnight," he said.

She heard him speaking to Mrs. Gibson-Brown on the landing downstairs, and then, a minute later, the sound of his car starting up in the street.

The Second Week

I

FREDA was having breakfast from a tray by her gas fire, when Mrs. Gibson-Brown knocked at the door early on Monday morning.

"Telephone, Miss Mackenzie," she called. "Are you up? Telephone."

"I'll be down in a second," Freda answered. She waited until she had heard the flapping of Mrs. Gibson-Brown's slippers descend the stairs. It was one of her unspoken rules that she was not seen in the morning before she was dressed. On the only occasion Freda had knocked at her door before half-past eight, she had been treated very distantly, as if she was intruding, and had not done the 'right thing'.

Certainly Mrs. Gibson-Brown did not look her best in a hair-net and the faded silk kimono patterned with pagodas and ladies with knitting-needles in their hair.

Freda knew that the door of the *salon* would be left open for her, and that Mrs. Gibson-Brown would be safely back in her bedroom.

Who can be 'phoning at this hour? she wondered.

It was Derek, cheerfully apologetic.

"I thought I'd give you a ring today," he said. "There didn't seem much point waitin' for tomorrow." He didn't waste any more time. "You busy tonight?"

"Yes, I am," answered Freda. "I have a lesson to prepare."

"That don't take all evening, does it? Can't I see you afterwards?"

"I shall be feeling rather tired by the time I've finished," she said.

"Oh! I was lookin' forward to seein' you." His voice sounded crestfallen.

Impulsively she thought of asking him to a meal.

"If you'd like to, you could come here for supper," she suggested. "If you don't think you would be bored. You could read or something, while I work."

As she said it she realized how stupid it was to invite him. Why had she done it? They had nothing in common, and it would cause raised eyebrows from her landlady if she saw Freda entertaining an ordinary sailor. But it was done now. She waited for his answer.

"Smashin'," said Derek enthusiastically. "What time can I come?"

"Seven?"

"Can't be too soon for me. Seven it is."

Whistling, Derek walked back from the 'phone box outside the William Tell to his home in Jubilee Road.

"Up early, ain't yer?" asked Joan over the banisters. Except for the first morning of his leave Derek had stayed in bed until ten at least.

"Go and get dressed," said Derek fastidiously. "Your 'air looks 'orrible."

He wandered into the kitchen.

"Goin' out to supper tonight, Mum," he couldn't resist telling her.

Mrs. Smith looked surprised. This was the first time he had volunteered information about his activities.

"Are yer?" she said.

Derek waited hopefully a moment, to see if she would show any interest, but she went on cooking the breakfast kippers.

"You know 'oo with?" he asked.

"No," said Mrs. Smith. " 'Oo?"

"Miss Mackenzie," said Derek triumphantly. Having said it he was immediately sorry.

"Go on!" said his mother. "Miss Mackenzie up the school?"

" 'S'right," said Derek. " 'Ere, Mum," he cautioned her. "I shouldn't 'ave told you really. Don't let on to Joan, will you?"

"I've forgotten what you told me already," said Mrs. Smith conspiratorially. "Dad!" she shouted. "Joan! Come and eat yer kippers while they're 'ot."

"Mum?" said Derek, after Joan and his father had left the house, and he was drying up the dishes. "Mum, you won't forget what I asked, will you?"

They were being more intimate than for a long time.

"No." Mrs. Smith was hurt. "I told yer, my lips is sealed." But she was overcome by curiosity. "What you doin' 'avin' supper with 'er, Derry?"

"She ask me," he said.

"You goin' out with 'er, then?" Mrs. Smith was at a loss.

"Sort of," answered Derek. "I seen 'er twice."

Mrs. Smith emptied the washing-up water out of the enamel bowl, and the water gurgled away down the scarred stone sink. "What she want with a boy like you?" she said.

"Perhaps she likes me," said Derek huffily. "Nothin' so funny in that, is there?"

"Seems queer to me," ruminated his mother. "She's got a boy, 'asn't she?"

Matthew's appearance was a piece of gossip Joan had brought home last term. "She's got a boy, our new teacher 'as. 'E come for 'er in a car."

"She may 'ave," said Derek indifferently. "I 'aven't asked." His voice was flat and toneless, and although Mrs. Smith was bursting with questions, she found she could no longer ask them. The barrier had descended again.

Derek picked up a newspaper and disappeared behind it, slouched in the kitchen chair. Mrs. Smith went on noisily swilling the sink.

"Mum?" he said after a while. "When you does the washin', dhobie my collar and vest, will you? I'll give 'em a press this afternoon."

This was the first occasion on his leave that Derek had surrendered his independence. She had tentatively offered to press his uniform, and he had nearly bitten her head off.

"We don't 'ave mothers when we're at sea," he snapped, "and we don't 'ave crumpled suits, neither."

He had been sorry afterwards and taken her to the pictures that afternoon to compensate.

Mrs. Smith was delighted to do any small chore for him.

"When you goin' out then?" she asked.

" 'Bout six," he said. Then with sudden goodwill, "I'll do Dad's suit while I'm at the iron, eh?"

"There. You look very nice." Mrs. Smith straightened Derek's collar for him, and he pulled his jumper down firmly over his hips before going to the mirror to put on his hat.

"Where you goin'?" asked Joan, looking up from the comic she had spread out on the table.

"If you ask no questions you'll get told no lies," said Mrs. Smith. "Your brother's goin' out, that's all."

"Not with Maureen Lacey, 'e ain't," said Joan. "Doris said 'e's dropped 'er."

"Oh, shu' up," Derek said irritably. He was ready to go. "Nobody wants your comments, thanks. S'long, Mum." He put his arms round her waist and kissed her. He was in high spirits.

" 'Ave a nice time," said Mrs. Smith, as she saw him to the door. "I don't understand it, Derry, but bein' young's the time to do what you want, I suppose."

" 'Bye, Mum," he said again. "Expec' me when you see me." He heard the bus coming and pelted up Jubilee Road to catch it. As he jumped on he turned to wave to his mother, but she had already gone indoors.

The bus was held up where the road was being repaired, and Derek cursed impatiently. Just my bleeding luck, he thought. He had never known a journey seem more tedious or slow.

Freda had given him instructions how to reach Bannerton Gardens, and when he came out of the Underground at Gloucester Road he found his way without difficulty. He was excited about seeing her, and curious too. What sort of place was it she lived in? Would he have to meet other people? Would Freda be different in her own home? It was a totally new experience for him. He had never in his life gone visiting this sort of house, and only had an indistinct mental picture built up from what he had seen in films and odd remarks from blokes like Fauntleroy.

He pushed open the heavy front door and found himself standing in a square of patterned light, not much larger than the doormat underfoot. The light came from the stained-glass windows either side of the porchway. There was a letter-rack at eye-level, with criss-crossed black tapes on green baize. Derek glanced at it, saw a letter addressed to Freda and with a proprietary gesture disengaged it from the tape and put it inside the front of his jumper, along with his cigarette packet. Facing him was another door, originally painted cream, but now buff-coloured and peeling. It was not locked either, and he opened it into the dark hallway, with its black-and-white-checked tiled floor. Here and there a tile was broken, or had been kicked loose. There was a push-button light that Freda had told him would last him all the way up to her flat if he hurried. When he pressed the switch there was a distant clicking from the timing mechanism.

To his relief he met no one as he bounded upstairs. He arrived on the third floor slightly breathless, at exactly one minute to seven.

As she listened to him coming up the stairs, Freda glanced at her clock and noted the time with amusement. She opened the door to him before he knocked.

"I heard you," she said. "What punctuality! Come in."

He followed her into the room and stood just inside the door, looking round. He was obviously rather impressed, yet at the same time it in no way fitted in with his preconceived ideas.

"What had you expected then?" asked Freda, following his train of thought.

"I dunno, not this. More luxurious I suppose, not so comfy."

Freda made a face.

"Derek, what a horrid description. Comfy."

"Why?" He didn't understand.

She let the question drop.

"Sit down, anyway. Make yourself at home."

He sat down on the edge of the armchair in front of the gas fire, then remembered her letter.

He fished it out of his jumper and handed it to her.

"I brought up a letter for you."

She opened it, but it was only a circular, and not very interesting.

"Are you hungry?" she asked, putting the envelope behind the clock on the mantelpiece.

"Yes," said Derek. "What is there? I'll 'elp you get it." He stood up, glad to be of use, and followed her into the kitchenette.

She took two lamb cutlets out of the meat-safe.

"Is this kitchen all yours?" he asked.

"Yes," Freda nodded.

He was delighted. "You got your own bathroom, too?"

"Yes, that's the other door. It's almost as small as this."

"What it is to be rich," said Derek, grinning.

"I'm far from rich," Freda said, upset. She felt ashamed of having both a bathroom and kitchen to herself.

"Well, you don't 'ave to wash in the sink, do you?" He wasn't pointing it out maliciously and turned his attention to the meal.

"We 'avin' potatoes?"

"They're on." She indicated the saucepan on the stove. "The salad's ready, I've only got to make a dressing. I thought we'd have fried chops and tomatoes. Is that all right for you?"

"I'll do the fryin'. You sit down." He picked up a knife and expertly slid a piece of cooking-fat into the frying pan, gently shaking it as the fat began to melt. "Everyone 'as to take their turn at cookin' on the mess-deck. You 'ave a rest." He elbowed her out of his way. "Go on, Freda, you've been workin' all day. I like doin' it."

"All right, then, but don't forget to rub the meat with this garlic. Look. I'm putting it here." She went back into the room and started to set the table. Derek, having overcome his initial embarrassment by doing something he was used to doing, talked to her while he cooked.

"You can come and see to the spuds now," he said. "They're done." He turned the cutlets skilfully.

Freda drained the potatoes into the dish with melted butter.

"You can take 'em in," said Derek. "I won't be a minute with this lot." He leant across her for a fork, and as he did so, his hair touched her forehead. He did not notice, but Freda was aware of the contact, and turned away quickly. He watched her as she mixed the salad dressing.

"What's that you're puttin' in?"

"Olive oil."

Derek looked doubtful. "We always 'ave salad cream at 'ome," he said.

"I think you'll like this." Freda carried the salad bowl into the sitting-room, and he followed her with the rest of the dishes. He was hungry and enjoying himself. He sat down and helped them both to the food.

"Enough potatoes? 'Ave you got any bread?"

"There's a loaf in the kitchen."

He fetched it, then looked round again, before sitting down.

"You 'aven't got any beer, I suppose?"

"Oh dear," said Freda. "It never entered my head. I've some sherry?"

"Let's 'ave some of that then."

She poured out two glasses.

"Take a sip from mine," said Derek. "Go on, it's an old naval custom. We call it sippers." He liked initiating her. "When we 'as our tot of rum every day the bloke dishin' it out 'as a sip from everyone's. You should see 'im when 'e's finished."

Freda obediently took a sip from his glass.

"'Ere," said Derek indignantly. "That's not sippers, that's gulpers. 'And it over while there's still some left."

After they had eaten, he leant back in the chair.

"Seems funny," he said meditatively, "you teachin' my sister. If I was a few years younger, you might be teachin' me, mightn't you?"

Freda put down her coffee-cup.

"I think that's what I'd like to do, Derek."

"What? Teach me?"

"Yes," Freda nodded. "You're intelligent and sensitive, but you've never had a chance to really appreciate things. I could do it for you, if you'd let me. Take you to films, concerts, exhibitions. I want to," she said.

She wasn't altogether coherent but Derek managed to follow.

"You mean you want to go *with* me to all those things?"

"Yes. I want to help you enjoy them."

Up till this moment Derek's relationships with women had been on two levels. Either they had been with girls like Maureen, who might or might not give him what he wanted, or they had been casual pick-ups, good for a turn after a couple of drinks. But Freda didn't fit into either category.

He wanted to make love to her, he thought, looking at her. He had realized that from the time he had waited for her outside the school. He was a matelot, and matelots thought of that primarily when they met any girl. But he didn't for a second think he had half a chance with Freda. How could he, with a girl like her?

Why go on seeing her, then? he asked himself. Was it in the hope of making love to her one day? Could it be because he liked her? He never contemplated just being friends, but he felt depressed at the thought of not spending most of his leave with her. He didn't think beyond his leave. He lived from moment to moment because he might at any time be sent away, possibly for years. Going out with her as she suggested would give him a chance to know her better. And besides, there might be something in it. Worth a try, anyway.

"Okay, teacher," he said. "Take me on."

The bargain had been struck, and Freda felt very happy about it.

"Let's wash up," she suggested, beginning to clear away the plates.

"I'll do the dishin' up for you," he offered, grinning. "'Dishin' up' was what they called it in the Andrew. Payment for my lessons. When do we start?"

But they did it together. Derek pulled off his jumper, and Freda was very conscious what a nice-looking boy he was. He had a well-proportioned face, the eyes wide apart and the mouth sensitive. His fair hair was streaked almost white in parts where it had been bleached by the Mediterranean sun. He was quick and thorough with the washing up, swabbing down the draining board, and scrubbing the sink.

"Now I have to work," said Freda. "You must amuse yourself." She sat down at the table with a history text-book and a sheaf of papers in front of her. Derek wandered over to the bookshelf and found himself something to read. He settled down, then looked at Freda. She seemed absorbed in her work.

"When do we start goin' out?" he asked again.

"I don't know," she said, looking up. "Don't interrupt me, Derek, there's a good boy."

"I'm not a good boy," he said, but he went back to his book. They were silent for a time. Suddenly Freda put down her pen.

"You'll have to go by ten," she said. "My landlady's narrow-minded."

"Blimey," said Derek disappointedly. "It's 'alf-past nine already. And all you've done the 'ole evenin's work."

"Oh, Derek," she said. "You knew perfectly well I was going to work. I told you this morning. It was the condition on which you came at all."

"I didn't think I'd be so chokka," he said. "Seein' you sittin' there lookin' pretty, and not bein' able to talk to you. I've been wantin' to kiss you," he said, "for the last 'alf-hour."

Freda was taken by surprise, but answered him firmly.

"That isn't in the curriculum, Derek."

"There's some things you don't 'ave to teach me," he said doggedly. He came over to where she was sitting and balanced himself on the wooden arm of her chair. "Some lessons sailors don't need to learn."

Firmly he put his hands on her shoulders and pulled her round to look at him. Then he took her face between both palms, his fingers in her hair, and holding her head back, kissed her. He kissed her in the way she might have expected, remembering how he had taken her books to carry them, and brought her letter up from downstairs. He kissed her again, with obvious experience.

"Oh, Derek," Freda said. "You know this means I can't go on seeing you, don't you?"

"Don't be bloody silly," said Derek, running his finger down the groove at the back of her neck. "It's got nothin' to do with the other thing. Don't you like makin' love?"

"Of course I do, that's beside the point. If I'm going to help you to understand and appreciate things you don't know about, it's no good having distractions."

"But it just makes it more fun for both of us," said Derek. "If I thought I was goin' to kiss you when we comes out of a theatre, I'd be able to sit through it much better." He was pleased by his own argument, and without giving her a chance to reply, kissed her again. "When do I see you next?" he demanded.

Freda was at her most vulnerable being kissed. I'm up to my neck in it now, she thought. She didn't want to respond to him, yet she couldn't help stroking the little golden hairs on his fore-arm.

"Wednesday," she said, giving herself a day. If she saw him tomorrow she knew she would never be able to re-establish the situation as it had been, without this distracting element of intimacy. But the day after tomorrow would give her time.

"Okay," he said. "I'll come 'ere again, shall I?"

"No," said Freda, knowing that would be fatal, "I'll meet you out. What shall we do?"

"Up to you, teacher." He was overwhelmed at his success.

"Well, you've seen a foreign film. How about a concert?"

"Yes, I never been to a concert," he said, not really caring.

"I'll get the tickets, shall I?"

"Yeah, you do that." He was content to leave the arrangements to her.

"We'll each pay for ourselves," Freda stipulated.

"No, we won't," said Derek. "My leave's only just begun, and I'm not broke yet. We'll talk about it when I am."

"But concerts can be expensive."

"I told you. I'll pay." He was annoyed. "Don't keep on about it."

Freda suddenly looked at the clock.

"Derek, you must go. It's ten, I daren't let you stay later."

He put on his collar and lanyard and jumper.

"Straighten my collar, will you?" he asked.

Freda had watched intrigued. "What a complicated uniform," she commented. She did as he asked, and he turned suddenly and held her, kissing her forehead.

"I'll see you Wednesday. Shall I pick you up at school?"

"No. I'd rather the girls didn't see us. I'll meet you at the Festival Hall at half-past seven or whenever the concert begins. You'll have to check from the papers. I will want to come back here and change."

"Change?" He looked worried. "What do I wear then?"

"Your uniform. That's perfectly all right, though one doesn't see many of them nowadays."

He was relieved, and crossed to the door.

"Goodnight, Freda. It's been a smashin' evening."

She called him back. "Derek, you won't tell Joan about us, will you?"

"Oh sure, I can't wait to do that. Thanks once again." He smiled at her, then winked as he closed the door. He pushed the light switch and ran down the stairs. Only ten o'clock. If he was quick he'd have time for a wet at the Red Shield before it closed.

Freda sat still for quite a while. She felt rather stunned at this sudden development in their relationship. She couldn't deny she found him very attractive physically. She could still feel the pressure of his hands on her shoulders and his mouth against her forehead. Somehow she could not continue her preparation of the history lesson. She undressed slowly and went to bed.

II

In the Red Shield, which he reached only about twenty minutes before closing time, Derek bumped straight into Johnnie Cooper, in the company of an elderly gentleman with a bald head.

"Smudge," cried Johnnie delightedly. "What do you know!"

Johnnie was in uniform too, but his cap was further on the back of his head than regulations allowed.

"This is my oppo," Johnnie told the elderly gentleman. "Derek Smith."

"Hallo, Smudge," said the elderly gentleman, who was quite *au fait* with service nicknames. "What can I get you?"

"Black and tan," said Derek. He had completely forgotten about Freda in his pleasure at meeting Johnnie. "I was goin' to look you up," he said, "but I 'adn't a moment. What've you been doin'?"

"Oh, the usual," said Johnnie. "My Mum's in 'ospital, so it ain't all sunshine at 'ome. The old man's as miserable as sin. I been to the dogs with 'im Saturday."

"Got yourself lashed up?" asked Derek, indicating the elderly gentleman, who was now coming back to them, carefully carrying Derek's pint.

"Yeah," said Johnnie, "I knew 'im before we went foreign. 'E's a poet bloke. Always good for a couple of quid but never stops yappin' about friendship."

"I won't muscle in then," said Derek. "Thanks," he added, taking his glass as the man rejoined them.

"I met Johnnie years ago," said the poet, "so we're quite old pals, aren't we, Johnnie?" He turned to Derek. "Johnnie knows I like to feel my friends in the navy don't just come up to see me for what they can get, but because they like my companionship too. Pick-ups are two a penny," he went on, "but I like to establish a basis of mutual trust and affection." As he spoke his eyes appraised Derek's broad shoulders.

The three of them conversed a moment or so more. Then Derek said, "I'll be pushin' off. When'll I see you, Johnnie?"

"I'm goin' out with Dad tomorrow," said Johnnie. " 'Ow about Wednesday? We'll 'ave a real booze-up."

"No, I can't see you Wednesday," said Derek, remembering. "Better make it Friday."

"Okay. Friday. 'Ere?"

"Yeah, this'll do. Goodnight," he said to the bald poet. "S'long, Johnnie."

"Goodnight," said the poet. "Johnnie has my 'phone number if you want it."

Derek went out into the familiar Piccadilly night, but resisting its temptations he went straight to the tube.

III

Freda had gone to the Festival Hall on Tuesday after school. It was an ideal programme for Derek's first concert, and she was lucky to get seats fairly close to the orchestra.

All that day Freda had been thinking about Derek. She tried to consider the matter seriously, but couldn't. She found herself staring into space, completely forgetting her class, or the staff room conversation. The very thought of him touching her hand excited her. Over and over again she revisualized the previous evening, from the moment his hair first brushed her forehead in the kitchen, until he had left her.

On Wednesday she woke up already thinking about the evening.

The day, surprisingly, went quickly. She hurried back after school, bathed, changed and then took the tube to Waterloo.

Derek had not expected her to look so well-groomed and attractive. Standing outside the main entrance, with the concert-goers eddying round him, he was becoming more and more ill at ease. He was glad to see Freda, although she seemed to be a part of the other people, rather than someone with whom he could feel at ease.

"You look lovely," he said miserably.

"Thank you." Freda was in high spirits. "Let's go in. Oh, look, Derek, there's the choreographer who's bringing his company here next month."

He didn't know what a choreographer was, and the sight of the suave dark man depressed him more than ever. Freda opened her handbag and gave him the tickets and they went in.

The simple spacious foyer with its occasional square of colour complementing the wood and stone and glass impressed him more than he would have admitted. Together they ascended the stairs to the main concert hall. He had not expected it to be so big from the outside and was excited by the brilliant lights, the sweeping expanse of ceiling and the contemporary décor, with the boxes flying out from the walls like the cars in a scenic railway. The orchestra began filing in and tuning up, odd phrases of music suddenly filtering through the murmur of the audience.

He bought a programme for them both and handed it to Freda. They were to hear a Rossini overture, a new tone poem receiving its first performance, a romantic piano concerto, and, following the interval, a Beethoven symphony.

"Explain it to me," said Derek.

"Well, there's not much to explain," Freda replied. "You probably know the music of the overture anyway. It's gay and light-hearted and meant to set the tone for the opera, but now of course it's played as a lively piece of music. No one has heard the tone poem after that," she continued, "it's being played for the first time, so we'll have to see what the programme notes say about it."

They read the notes together, then looked round at the audience, and Freda pointed out several celebrities to him, including an American film-star, at whom he stared with great interest.

"She don't look anythin' like what she does in the films," he said, disappointed, after his prolonged scrutiny.

The leader of the orchestra entered and was received by a little burst of clapping. A pause, carefully timed, thought Freda, then the conductor strode in, tall and immaculate. He acknowledged the applause, turned and raised his baton; a drum roll which became a rumbling noise as the seats were raised and the audience stood for God Save the Queen. The anthem was performed theatrically, the tympanist sweeping the cymbals together in two great tangential arcs, the sound shimmering across the hall a split second afterwards. Another rumbling as the audience sat and settled themselves, a fluttering of programmes, and a coughing and clearing of throats. The conductor waited, pointedly, arms folded across his chest. Then, with the same swift, elegant movement he once more raised his baton. Simultaneously the auditorium lights dimmed, leaving the orchestra still brilliantly lit from above. A moment of suspension, then the downbeat of the baton, and the strings swept into the familiar opening melody of the overture.

Derek sat watching intently. Freda glanced at him once or twice and smiled at his concentration. He's trying hard, anyway, too hard to enjoy himself, she thought. But he joined in the applause at the end with enthusiasm.

"Yes," he said. "I 'ad 'eard it before, but never played like that. Them blokes with the fiddles didn't 'alf 'ave to work 'ard," he continued. "I should think their arms felt like droppin' off!"

Freda laughed. "Quite probably," she said. "This conductor has a reputation for driving the orchestra like slaves."

The tone poem, which followed, was, according to the programme notes, inspired by a day the composer had spent in London. Derek liked that music too, and was amused at the inclusion of bell-chimes and the simulation of ships' sirens and taxi horns by various brass and woodwind instruments.

"You could almost imagine you was standin' down by the docks," he said, happily identifying the sound pictures with the visual images of his own locality.

The concerto was one of three or four which had become immensely popular during the war. The soloist was a woman wearing a lilac-coloured evening dress with a low neckline. She played well, tackling the technical difficulties with ease, and accentuating the dramatic rhythms and melancholy Slavonic themes so that Freda, who was over-familiar with the work, found herself enjoying it as if she was hearing it for the first time. It occurred to her that its romanticism was just right for the occasion.

They went out during the interval, Freda leading the way to the big glass-fronted façade in order to show Derek the magnificent view of the river. He disliked her taking the lead this way.

"Want a drink?" he asked, trying to reassume the initiative.

"I'll have coffee," said Freda, thinking of the price of the seats.

"Well, I'm goin' to 'ave a drink," Derek answered shortly, "so you 'ave one, too. It's easier."

"I'll have a tomato juice, then."

They walked downstairs to the main bar, and Derek watched the people with interest. He was aware, too, that they were looking at him. A sailor was an unfamiliar sight in the concert hall. It was more common to see an evening dress, or a duffle-coat, but seldom a uniform. He felt less uncomfortable now. A bar, anywhere, made him feel at home. Freda stood back from the crowd trying to get drinks, and he pushed through the crush to order for them both.

"Good-evening," said a voice in his ear. "I didn't know you were interested in music."

Derek spun round.

"Faunty. Well I'll be . . ." He slapped his old messmate on the shoulder. "All dressed up, ain't you?"

Fauntleroy was wearing a dinner jacket which had been his father's several years before, and was a little short at the wrists.

"Come and meet my mother," he said, vaguely indicating the crowd, with the sherry glass in his hand. "Are you alone?"

"No," said Derek, "I'm with my girl."

They took their drinks towards the main part of the foyer. Fauntleroy disappeared between two American women discussing music in loud enthusiastic voices. They parted for Fauntleroy to thread his way between them, and for a moment he became obscured by the crowd.

"Who was that?" asked Freda, coming over to Derek, and slipping her arm through his.

"That's Fauntleroy, a bloke from *Dragon*, same mess as I was. 'E's with 'is mother. Let's get goin' before we 'ave to talk to 'er." He looked round for a way of escape, but it was too late.

"May I introduce my mother?" said Fauntleroy. "This is Derek Smith, Mother, from my mess, and . . ." he paused.

"My name's Freda Mackenzie," Freda said, terrified that Derek wouldn't perform the introduction adequately. But he conducted it with surprising ease.

"I don't know your name," he said to Fauntleroy, "so I can't introduce you properly."

"Michael McEwan," Fauntleroy said. He addressed himself to Freda. "Are you enjoying it?"

"Very much," she said. "Derek's never been to a concert before. It's a good programme to begin with, isn't it?"

"Indeed yes," said Fauntleroy, obviously trying to fathom their relationship. Derek had said 'My girl', but surely . . . ? "Personally I didn't go overboard for the tone poem. I'm not keen on descriptive pieces, are you?"

Derek, fuming with rage at having had himself referred to in such a patronizing way, and then not being able to defend his own taste, found himself beside Fauntleroy's mother.

She was a thin, flat-chested woman who had once been pretty. Now her hair was grey, however, she lacked colour. The evening dress she wore was dark blue lace, the sort of long shapeless gown worn by ladies of the English middle classes year after year. She had on a triple row of cultured pearls, and her hands were red and not well shaped. Freda noticed this and thought, no maid since the war. It was something equivalent to her own background.

"Do you like the navy?" Mrs. McEwan asked Derek. "How much of your two years have you done?"

"Two?" said Derek scornfully. "I'm not a National Serviceman. I'm regular. I done four already."

Freda found Fauntleroy pleasant but lacking in humour.

"Very much a Mummy's boy," she said to Derek as they went up the stairs again, summoned by the mellow interval-gong.

"I think 'e's queer," said Derek knowledgeably, "but 'e don't know it."

During the symphony which followed Derek seemed a little restless, fidgeting with the programme and staring round the hall. But in the finale the expertly timed actions of the drummer, darting from one percussion instrument to the other, re-engaged Derek's attention, and he was caught up in the exciting momentum of the movement. When it was over and the conductor returned for the third time and they stood applauding, Freda asked him how he had enjoyed it.

"I liked the concerto best," said Derek. "I'd 'eard it on the films before, but I didn't know there was so much of it."

Freda talked to him about the music as they mingled with the crowd streaming from the hall.

"It won't be such an ordeal next time," she assured him. "The more you hear the easier it becomes."

But she had the feeling he wasn't listening very intently. He guided her through the people until they were opposite Waterloo Station. Then he suddenly hailed a taxi.

" 'Op in," he said. "You don't want to spoil the evenin' by goin' in the tube."

In the taxi he put his arm along the back of the seat and kissed her with more sureness than he had done on Monday.

"I always like it better," said Freda, "when I know how a person kisses, even though it's more exciting the first time. First kisses can be so awfully disappointing."

He was very surprised at her saying so. He'd never known a girl tell him things like that before. Kids like Maureen always pretended sex didn't exist, even when they were having it, and the other sort never bothered to say anything at all. Freda seemed to be actually enjoying herself. He'd never thought girls of her class would.

He directed the driver along Bannerton Gardens.

"Just 'ere, on the right, Driver, by the lamp-post." He paid with a flourish. "G'night, Driver," he said courteously.

"G'night, Mate," said the cabman. Derek came into the porch-way, inside the front door, with Freda.

"I suppose I can't come up?" he asked.

Her head was against the letter-rack, and he kissed her.

"No," she said. "I daren't risk it." She tried to push him away. "I must go up, now, Derek."

"I want to make love to you properly," he said. It was a line he had used before. At this point it rarely failed.

"Well, you're not going to." She straightened up, and held him back by putting her hands against the rough blue serge of his upper arms. "Goodnight." She relaxed against him, slipping her hands round the back of his neck, coming into contact with the smooth cotton collar.

Reluctantly he let her go.

"Tomorrow?" he asked.

"All right," she agreed without argument.

"Do we 'ave to go out again? Can't I come 'ere?"

She hesitated.

"I won't make love to you, I promise. You can read poetry to me for all I care."

"Very well."

He moved to kiss her again.

"No. Or I'll never get upstairs. Come here round about five-thirty."

"Okay." He opened the inner door for her. "Goodnight."

She walked a yard or so along the hall, and he pressed the electric light button for her, and the mechanism started its clicking.

"Go on up to your flat, or you won't be fit to go teachin' my sister in the mornin'!"

He closed the door quietly behind him.

IV

Derek slept late on Thursday morning. He had walked a good part of the way home the night before, not because there was any real need, for the buses still ran after midnight even if they were not frequent, but because after leaving Freda he wanted to think things over.

I can't make her out, he said to himself. I can't make out what she wants. When he kissed her she was so relaxed and sexy, but other times she was distant and unbending, always turning moments of intimacy into little lectures, separating them by her patronizing attitude.

His desire to make love to her had increased. He wanted to subdue her school-teacher priggishness with his own animal vitality, but he arrived home without any idea of how he was going to do it.

Mrs. Smith brought him his breakfast in bed in the morning.

"Thanks, Mum." He sat up immediately with no lingering sleepiness, used to abrupt awakenings to go on watch.

"Your leave's 'alf gone, ain't it?" she said, putting the tray down on the uneven bumps of his knees.

It was not until his mother had left the room that he was suddenly aware how important the last week or so of his leave had become to him. Usually by this time he was so bored by being home that he was quite happy to contemplate rejoining his ship, and once he had even returned two days early, because his leave pay had run out. Now he realized he had only ten days in which to work things out with Freda, and that didn't seem long enough.

Later in the morning he walked past the school on his way to the pub, and thought of her inside the building. He visualized her writing on a blackboard, her arm stretched up to reach it, exposing the curve of her breast. As he turned down to the William Tell, he indulged in a series of erotic thoughts, so that by the time he pushed open the door of the Public Bar, with its chipped gilt letters, his eyes were adrenalin-bright, and he wished it was already half-past five, and he was running up the stairs to her flat. He stayed drinking rather late.

"Given up eatin'?" asked Mr. Frost.

"No." Derek stood up a little unsteadily. "Just thinkin'. Dinner will 'ave to wait for me today. Be seein' you."

In the street he came face to face with Maureen Lacey. It was impossible to pretend he had not seen her, so he stopped and said, "'Allo, Maur."

"'Allo, Derek." There was an awkward silence.

"You gettin' on all right?" she asked, making an effort to appear natural.

She had blushed when they had met, and now she looked miserable. Poor kid, he thought without arrogance. He couldn't help comparing her clothes with Freda's. Without realizing it the things he would have considered smart and fetching before now seemed wrong. He didn't like her long ear-rings with their pink glass stones, or her red open-toed shoes.

"You doin' anything after dinner?" he asked.

"No." It was Thursday, her half-day.

"Come and 'ave a cup of tea up the Park Caff then. I'll see you there 'alf two." He intended to give her the brush-off in the kindest way he could.

After dinner he set off happily. He'd talk to Maureen, then go on over to Freda's. It meant he wouldn't have to hang around doing nothing all afternoon.

He coincided with Maureen on the wide pavement outside the café, and they went in together and sat at a corner table.

"Somethin' to eat?" he asked.

"No thanks."

"Just tea then?"

She nodded, and he beckoned to the waitress who was abstractedly chewing gum. "Two teas, Miss."

She brought them slopped in the saucers. Derek leant his elbows on the glass-topped yellow table and put his chin in his hands.

"Maur?"

"Yes, Derry?" She moved the full ashtray to the edge of the table for something to do with her hands.

"Maur, I got to talk to you."

"Yes?" She had undone her coat and with a feeling of guilt he saw she still wore his photograph in her locket.

"I 'aven't seen much of you this leave," he said.

"No." She did not help him.

"It's no good fallin' for a sailor," he said. "We just can't stay steady."

Her eyes filled with tears. He put his hand over hers.

"Don't cry, Maur. You mustn't be un'appy over me. There's lots of other boys you can go with."

"I want you," she said. "I waited all the time you was away." She was suddenly vicious. "You got someone else, ain't you?"

He nodded. "Yes I 'ave." He said it unwillingly.

"You goin' to marry 'er?"

"No. I told you, matelots like a change."

"I waited all that time," said Maureen. "I didn't even let another boy kiss me."

"It's no good keep sayin' that," said Derek. "That was your own lookout, wasn't it?"

Maureen took out her handkerchief. "I'm sorry, Derry. I didn't mean to say that. I know it puts you off."

"It doesn't put me off," he said irritably. "I told you, it's because I've got someone else."

"Does she live round 'ere?" asked Maureen. It hurt her to ask for details but her masochistic curiosity forced her to question him.

"No, she lives up West." Derek gave that information gladly. That would keep her off the track.

Maureen finished her tea. "I'm goin' now, Derry."

He stood up. "D'you mind if I don't see you back? I'll stay and 'ave another cup."

"No." She shook her head.

"No 'ard feelin's," he asked.

"Not really," said Maureen. Her eyes filled again. "Oh, Derry . . ."

The waitress leant on the bar counter and stared at them curiously, still chewing vigorously with her mouth open.

"Yes?" he said.

"If you ever want me back . . ."

It was a bit dramatic, he thought, like a film. He waited for her to add "I'll always be there," but she didn't. Instead she buttoned up her coat and hurried out of the café. Derek sat down again.

"Miss," he called.

The girl came over to him.

"Clear away this lot and bring us some more tea."

"Broken another 'eart, Jack?" she said, still chewing.

He didn't answer.

V

He was at Gloucester Road long before five-thirty. At ten past five he took up a position outside the Underground to catch Freda on her way out.

"Hallo, Derek." It was she who took him by surprise. "Waiting for someone?"

He took her arm and she stiffened slightly.

"No, Derek, not here."

"Okay, okay." He shrugged, although inwardly he was offended. But as they walked up Bannerton Gardens, Freda said, "You see, I was right. There's my landlady."

Mrs. Gibson-Brown came towards them, with a slightly tottering step because of her pointed court-shoes with their high curved heels.

"Good afternoon, Miss Mackenzie," she said, and her eyes took in Derek curiously. There was no mistaking it. He wasn't the right class. Then she nodded to him distantly. "Good afternoon."

"'Afternoon," mumbled Derek. "Made me feel as if I was somethin' the cat brought in," he said to Freda as they turned into the porched doorway.

Up in her flat, keeping to his promise, he made no attempt to kiss her. Freda couldn't help feeling a sense of disappointment. She would have liked him to have tried, even if only to remind him of his undertaking, and also because she had a sudden fear that she might no longer be attractive to him.

Completely at home now Derek made a pot of tea, and as they sat drinking it he asked her rather diffidently if he might, now and then, have a bath in her flat.

"We 'aven't got one at 'ome," he said, "so I goes down to the public ones. I could come 'ere when you're at school per'aps?"

"You can have one now if you like," Freda offered. "I'll mark some books. Go on," she urged, noticing his hesitation, for having asked the favour, Derek's pride now made him wish he hadn't, "You'll find a clean towel in the cupboard."

"Thanks then." He stood up and took off his jumper. It was a very tight fit and difficult to remove. He managed to get it halfway over his head, then asked Freda to assist him. "Give us an 'and to get this off, would yer please?" His directions came muffled comically from inside the thick wool. "Pull from the bottom 'ard."

Suddenly the jumper peeled over his broad shoulders and his dishevelled head appeared, his face flushed with the exertion.

"Bloody silly uniform," he said. "I'd like to get my 'ands on the bloke what thought it up." He folded the jumper elaborately and laid it on a chair. "Where d'you say the towel was?"

"In the cupboard. I'll get it for you."

"No, don't bother. You stay still. I can find my own way."

"Bathroom's along the corridor in the North wing," said Freda.

Derek laughed and pushed open the door. The kitchen and bathroom doors were separated by a wall space of not more than two yards, and the intervening wall was a partition of thin matchboard that Mrs. Gibson-Brown had had put up when the house was converted.

Derek turned on the tap and Freda heard the key turn.

"I've taken the blue towel," he shouted, above the noise of the running water.

"Very suitable," Freda called back. She began to mark her class's compositions, and went through them to find Joan Smith's first. "I'm just marking your sister's book," she said. "You can see it when you come out." The composition was called 'If I won a football pool'. Joan, like two-thirds of the class, wanted to go to Hollywood and meet the stars. The rest of the money, she said, she'd give to Mum and Dad. Only one girl, who had a crush on Freda and wanted to please her, wrote that her winnings would go entirely to charity.

"I won't be long," Derek answered. He had turned off the tap and Freda could hear him scrubbing vigorously. "This ain't 'alf luxury."

"Not really," said Freda. "The bath's too short for me. It must be agony for you."

It wasn't long before the door opened and Derek came out looking fresh and clean, with his hair watered down, like a little boy going to a party. He wore only his bell-bottoms now, and the blue towel round his neck.

"Sorry to be a nuisance," he said, "but I've gone and cut my 'and on a ruddy nail by the door."

"Where?" said Freda. "Let me see?"

He held out his hand and she moved a step to take it, but before she had touched him he was holding her in an iron hug.

"Forgive the dirty trick," he said. "But I figured out it was the best approach." He kissed her hair, then her mouth.

"Oh, Freda, I want you so much. I thought about nothin' but you since I see you last night."

The warmth of his naked arms and chest excited her. He was sunburned and smooth-skinned and his body was hard.

"You're so different, Freda."

"You are too."

They were so close that each could feel the slight trembling of the other, and they stood together for some moments not kissing or speaking. Then Derek held her away from him, and began to unfasten her dress. To Freda, at that moment, there seemed not the slightest reason to stop him.

"Is there an ashtray 'andy?" asked Derek. He raised himself on his elbow and stretched out his other arm to put the ashtray on the bedside table nearer to him. In this difficult position, leaning across Freda, he managed to take a cigarette out of the blue and white packet, and light it. Then his arm gave way and he rolled back beside her.

"It had to happen, didn't it?" said Freda. She thought she ought to feel guilty. Why don't I? she asked herself, what could be more immoral, I don't love him at all, I just wanted him. But that seemed a justification in itself. She felt she knew now how love affairs began. It was like this. You wanted someone so much there was nothing you could do about it unless you had the sort of super-human self-control that made people into nuns and saints. It was a physical demand, so strong, that when it presented itself here and now in the form of Derek, it was impossible to deny. Reason, restraint were swept aside. It could happen in spite of one's moral precepts. Yet somehow, to her, it was more than animal lust, or the pursuit of bodily sensation, and she felt she was doing nothing wrong or disgraceful.

Derek was suddenly overwhelmed with affection for her. Before, she had been a school teacher, or a sophisticated young woman, always a cut above him, even when they kissed. Now, naked, the situation was reversed. He dominated. Poetry, music, the theatre, counted for nothing. What mattered were lips and neck and thighs, his strength, her submissiveness.

"You know the time?" he asked her lazily, his arm still under her shoulders.

"No, tell me?" Her voice was drowsy.

"Nine nearly."

"Oh, poor Derek. You must be starving."

In a second she was out of bed, before he had had time to hold her back.

"I'd just as soon 'ave you to eatin'."

She laughed, pleased, and wrapped her dressing-gown round her, slipping her feet into little straw mules.

"I bet you got those in Italy. Didn't you?"

"Yes. Eggs?"

"Smashin'." He lay back, listening to the catch of the cupboard opening, closing, the fat beginning to hiss in the pan, the sound of the plates and the cutlery.

"Come and help," demanded Freda.

He stretched, and sitting on the edge of the bed, began to dress. Freda came to the kitchen door.

"I can't resist you like that."

"You'd better," said Derek with a grin. "We don't want no burnt eggs."

She came over and kissed him, then as he responded too quickly, she laughed and released herself, and went back to the stove.

"Gosh, I was 'ungry," said Derek, finishing his eggs and wiping the plate round with a piece of bread.

"Look at the clock," said Freda. "It's ten to ten."

He drained his cup and held out his arms to her.

"I'll give you a ring," he said. "I'll probably see you tomorrow."

"Yes, do that. You don't know how much I don't want you to go."

"As much as I don't want to, neither."

He held her tighter.

"Derek. It's ten. You must go."

He kissed her for the last time. "I'm going now. Goodnight, Freda. And thanks."

He said the 'thanks' as if it had been expected of him, and it embarrassed her, almost upset her. She didn't want Derek to think she was granting him a favour.

"Goodnight, Derek." She smiled at him affectionately. After all, Derek probably thought he was being polite. She doubted whether he thanked his Mile End girls for whatever they gave him in the way of sexual privileges. The 'thanks' had been in deference to her class.

"See you."

He was gone, the door slammed behind him, his footsteps echoed on the stairs.

Freda poured herself out another cup of coffee and crossed her fingers that he wouldn't bump into Mrs. Gibson-Brown.

I won't go home this weekend, she decided. I'll stay with Derek instead. His leave is so short, I must be with him all I can. She was more delighted, more curious, more amused by Derek than she remembered being by any person in her life. He was unspoiled and generous and humorous, she told herself, so that Matthew, who had been her interest for so long, seemed jaded and dull. Making love to him had been inevitable. Now, in their new relationship as lovers, as well as pupil and teacher, she would be able to help him more than ever.

When she had finished her coffee she went down to the *salon* and sent a wire home to her mother.

All day at school on Friday, Freda found life diverting and gay. The girls delighted her, and the ponderousness of Mr. Pethcart and the studied broadmindedness of the single-minded Miss

Parrot made them seem as stylized as characters from Dickens. The hours flew. It was playtime, and then it was dinner. Dinner duty was not in the least boring. The noise and the smell and the scuffling in the queue which twisted between the twelve long bare tables simply made Freda's warmth towards humanity increase. She corrected the bad manners without irritation. In the past she had despaired at these bleak mealtimes, at the children furtively feeding themselves with their fingers, at the hurried stacking of plates, so that the unfinished potatoes would ooze between them, the meat thrown on to, and then trodden in to, the floor.

Freda walked between the tables, theoretically supervising, until she was standing by Joan Smith. The rest of the table began to eat with ostentatious politeness, but Freda wasn't interested in them today.

"How's your brother getting on?" she asked Joan, longing to talk about Derek, however obliquely.

Her afternoon lessons went well, and at half-past four she didn't linger at all, but hurried home to await the telephone call from Derek. He's bound to want to see me tonight, she thought. She changed her dress and sat down to read a book, but couldn't concentrate. Was that the 'phone? But it must have been for Mrs. Gibson-Brown or the girl in the flat downstairs, because no one came to call her.

At seven o'clock she decided not to wait supper for him. I can easily cook something for him if he wants it, she decided. He's probably had his tea at about six and won't be hungry. But he still hadn't called by eight, or eight-thirty, or nine.

The telephone rang again, and with a curious aching in her stomach, as if she'd gone without food, Freda heard Mrs. Gibson-Brown shout up the stairs to her.

"Are you in, Miss Mackenzie? Telephone for you."

Deliberately, Freda waited a moment before she went down to the *salon*, and even a moment more before she picked up the receiver and spoke as normally as she could.

"Darling," said her mother's voice, distant across the wires from Kent. "I got your telegram. You're not ill, are you? I was worried. It isn't like you not to come home at the last minute like this."

"No," said Freda, so disappointed she could easily have cried. "I'm not ill. I've simply got a party tomorrow night, that's all."

"Oh, I'm so relieved," said her mother. "I didn't like to think of you all alone there, not well." They talked for a moment or two, Freda trying to keep the irritation out of her voice.

"There are the pips," she said with relief, "I'll see you as usual next week. Love to Daddy."

Slowly she went back to her gas fire. It's half-past nine, she said to herself. He knows he can't come here after ten. What can have happened? A feeling of something akin to humiliation was creeping over her. She'd given herself to him and now he'd dropped her. True he hadn't said he'd ring tonight, but she'd been so certain he would. Something had cropped up to stop him 'phoning. She tried to imagine predicaments which would get in his way. What did the girls at school say when they had been absent? Mum's ill and I had to look after our Ron. I had to go up to our Gran's to help her. Or had she done something to upset him? She began to go through their conversation in detail. Then she looked at the clock. It was five past ten.

He'll 'phone in the morning, she thought, unless he thinks I have gone home for the weekend. In that case he may not ring till Monday. She knew she was giving him excuses for the now seeming possibility that he would fail her tomorrow, and Sunday too. Yet how could he break with her so abruptly, no telephone call, no contact at all, when only a few hours before, they had experienced the ultimate contact, the final intimacy? It seemed incredible to think that since last night, when they had established between them a relationship which must surely have dimmed all other relationships by its intensity, he was able now totally to disregard it.

All the elation of the day had gone. She began to argue with herself about him, to justify her own actions. Without his presence, his charm and physical attractiveness faded, and his faults began to grate on her. She remembered small things, such as the way he had mopped his plate automatically with bread, how he had said 'thanks' at the end of the evening as if she were a tart.

How can I have been so bowled over by physical desire? she asked herself. I was crazy. Apart from that there's no common ground on which Derek and I can meet at all. She was more used to his type of person than most of her class, her initial easiness was explained by that. Since she had started teaching she did not question class any more. It did not come into her head. People were nice or they were not nice. She wouldn't expect to find Derek at a cocktail party, or Matthew at the Jubilee Road Baths, but apart from that people fitted into their own background, and she thought no more about it. One had different values, different standards of judging. The attitude of the Mrs. Gibson-Browns of the world was beyond her. Or was it? One can take classlessness just so far, she decided, and no further. If Derek thought as I did he would have 'phoned me by now. She remembered quite clearly the time before she had started teaching and felt class difference far more distinctly than now. "Men will sleep with waitresses," she had said, "but no middle-class woman would sleep with a waiter. It's a totally different attitude to sex."

She sat thinking until after eleven, and then, with flatness and anticlimax, she went to bed.

In the morning, however, she awoke with renewed hope, and was quite lighthearted. Derek hadn't rung by eleven, and so she took the risk of going out to do some shopping. She hurried as much as she could, buying her things in the Gloucester Road, instead of going up to Kensington High Street to the better shops. She was back at her flat within half an hour, but there was no message on her door to say anyone had 'phoned.

Derek did not ring all afternoon, and at half-past five, rather despising herself, she rang Matthew at his digs.

"I'm in town this weekend," she said. "Any chance of tonight?"

"Of course." Matthew was not displeased. "If you don't mind a foursome. I promised to go to the cinema with Eleanor and Bob. But I should love you to come too."

"You'll fetch me then?" Freda tried to sound enthusiastic.

"Yes. Seven-thirty. We're not eating first, probably a sandwich afterwards."

At a quarter past seven, when she was almost ready to leave, Derek telephoned her. His voice sounded slurred, but it was difficult to be sure.

"Freda? Can I see you tonight?"

"I'm sorry, Derek. You've left it too late. I've made other arrangements now." She didn't mean to be cold. After all, he had made no promises to speak to her before. "I expected you to ring yesterday." Her tone was both nagging and possessive.

"When can I see you then?" asked Derek. "Tomorrow?"

I ought to say no, Freda thought. I must say no, or he'll take it for granted he can see me when he wants. But the sound of his voice dismissed all her wisdom.

"Tomorrow," she said, the happiness flooding into her own voice. "Come as early as you like."

From outside in the street came three hoots from Matthew's car.

"I must go," she said. "Come in the morning. We'll spend the day together." She could hear a piano playing in the background. "Are you in a pub?"

"'S'right. Can't keep anything from you, can I?" Derek was almost sentimental.

Matthew's horn sounded again impatiently. Six hoots this time. Freda said goodbye, ran up to her flat for her gloves, ran down again to the street. She arrived breathless at the car, looking flushed and excited.

"We're meeting the others at the cinema," said Matthew, as they drove off. "Freda, you're looking extremely pretty." And he kissed her on the cheek. "I'm a good driver," he said. "I make love to my women and watch the road at the same time."

VI

Derek had thought about Freda on Friday quite as much as Freda had thought about him. It was ridiculous that she was only a few hundred yards away from his home, and yet he couldn't see her, even wave. We ought to have a signal, he thought. But he remembered in a moment that the windows of the school building gave no view of the street, only the slate tops of the houses the other side of Jubilee Road.

The morning followed the usual pattern of all the days of

his leave. Breakfast, hang about until the pub opened, a pint or two and then dinner. There were little variations, sometimes his mother would send him on an errand, or he would do an odd job for her in the house, cleaning the grate or painting the framework of a door. But today he was impatient to see Freda again, and he made himself unapproachable and moody, so that his mother would leave him alone.

After dinner he slept in the kitchen chair, not because he was tired but to quicken the tedious progress of the afternoon. He could fall asleep and wake up again like an animal. If he was bored, and conditions favourable, he would sleep until there was something worth being awake for. And then he'd be fresh and alert in a second.

When, at half-past four he stretched and stood up, he realized that that evening he was meeting Johnnie Cooper at the Red Shield. I'll see him for an hour or so, he decided, then I'll give Freda a call round about eight.

In spite of the fact that he had wanted to see Freda all day, he didn't mind delaying the pleasure a little for the other pleasure of having a wet with his oppo. He had missed Johnnie, for Johnnie made him laugh. He could make the whole mess-deck have bellyache laughing.

He met Johnnie a few moments after opening time, and already the bars were beginning to fill. In came the soldiers, the sailors, an occasional girl with her friend, pushing towards the bar, pushing away again to the wooden seats along the wall, filtering down to the saloon, overtures for early pick-ups tentatively extended.

Derek and Johnnie wedged themselves at the end of the bar and started yarning. Sometimes they bought their own drinks, sometimes they were bought for them. "What's yours, Jack?" Their company changed, but always they were part of a group.

Derek had completely forgotten about Freda now. At half-past eight, when Johnnie said, "I'll ring up that poet bloke," Derek was ready for any skylark under the sun, and they went down into the Underground, free from cares. In the 'phone booth, Johnnie, in spite of his apparent *savoir faire*, became stricken with embarrassment, and tried to force the receiver into Derek's hand. They were laughing and scuffling when at the other end a voice answered them.

"Go on," said Derek. "Push the bloody button." The pennies clattered.

"'Allo?" said Johnnie, in his most formal voice. "Is that the residence of Mr. Paul Connaught?"

"It is."

"Can I speak to 'im?"

"Speaking."

"Oh, this is Johnnie, you know. I was with you Monday night. Johnnie."

Arrangements were made. "I got my oppo with me. (Okay, Smudge, if we meet 'em for a wet?) Yeah, okay, see you at the Rob Roy later on."

"We might as well go," said Johnnie, as they came up again into the thronging street, "if nothin' else don't turn up."

The Rob Roy was a tavern off Shaftesbury Avenue, famous for its Edwardian décor, the hundreds of photographs of stage stars, the old music-hall bills; famous, too, for Davy, the Welshman who owned it, thin as a lathe and hair the colour of golden syrup, although his eyebrows were quite grey. Sometimes in the summer he poured cold tea into a saucer, soaked a piece of cottonwool in the liquid, and dabbed it on his face to simulate a sun-tan. His wit, though of a stereotyped kind, was legendary. Davy's mother had been at the Rob Roy before him. Her funeral had been attended by half the theatre world of London. There had even been a wreath from royalty, and plenty of tributes from the West End's disreputable down-and-outs. A piano was played continuously all evening in the corner, anything you liked to ask for, Claire de Lune or Underneath the Arches, or something from the latest show.

Johnnie's poet was waiting for them, with Rupert who directed films and knew all the stars.

"Go on," said Johnnie. "Don't tell me you met Ava?"

But yes, the gentleman had even met Ava at a film festival at Cannes.

"We been to Cannes," said Johnnie, an apt conversationalist. "Do you know the Three Aces?"

At half-past ten the Rob Roy closed. Most of the servicemen went over to the Load of Hay across the road which stayed open till eleven, but Paul said, "Come back to my place and we'll open a bottle of whisky."

So they drove to Mayfair in Paul's big American car and went up to his flat somewhere behind Shepherd's Market. It was a small flat, and extremely elegant. The walls were fashionably papered and there was a collection of patchboxes, and another of eighteenth-century drawings. Paul's own volumes of poetry, specially bound in dark red morocco, stood on the mantelpiece between two jade lions.

Derek felt enormous and clumsy and terrified that he would break a glass or knock over one of the tiny polished tables. Mum should see that polish, he thought. He sat in the most solid armchair there was, and drank his whisky each time his glass was filled by Rupert or by Paul. It wasn't one bottle of whisky as far as he could count. It was three at least.

He was beginning to feel sleepy, then he knew he was going to be sick.

"Oh dear, *not* on my mushroom carpet," he heard Paul say. "Johnnie, do take him to the loo, there's a boy."

Derek stood up and stumbled to the door, leaning on Johnnie, or perhaps it was Rupert, or maybe he was walking alone and leaning on the doorway itself.

" 'Old on till we gets you there," said Johnnie through the haze. Johnnie could give the whole mess-deck the bellyache laughing Johnnie could, bellyache—the whole mess-deck bellyache—— He knew nothing more until he woke up in a strange but comfortable bed with the sun streaming on to his face and hurting his eyes.

"Breakfast?" asked Paul, who was standing immaculate at the foot of the bed, wearing a dark grey suit and a pearl on his lavender tie. "Or should I say lunch?"

"Where's Johnnie?" Derek sat up. "What's the time?"

"About one-thirty. Johnnie went an hour ago. He was going to the hospital with his Dad."

"Blimey, my head," said Derek.

"Look," Paul was quite business-like. "I've got to go out of town directly I've had a spot of lunch. Stay and have some with me, then wash it up. I'll trust you to lock the place. Okay?"

"Fine," said Derek. "Sorry about last night." He felt very ashamed—sick in *this* joint!

"You passed out, old chap," said Paul. "Fortunately there were three of us here to put you to bed." He went to the door. "There should be a dressing-gown in the cupboard. Have lunch first, and then take a bath when you've cleared up. I'll go and fix something."

There was game pie, and plenty of beer. Derek's head was better, but he wasn't really sober. Time seemed not to exist any more. It was dinner time, but it could have been early morning or late afternoon. The day didn't seem to have caught on for him.

After Paul had gone he washed up leisurely and bathed and dressed and drank some more beer. Paul's bathroom was black marble and the soap was pink. His beer was very potent.

For an hour or two Derek sat and dozed in a chair, and then the telephone rang and startled him. He didn't intend to answer it, but the caller had no intention of giving up. Derek swore. He took up the receiver. Anything to quieten the something row. It was Johnnie.

"Still there, mate? I'm on my way to the Rob Roy. Coming down?"

"Okay," said Derek. He might as well.

He locked the front door as Paul had instructed him and put the key through the letter box. Then he walked down to Piccadilly and up Shaftesbury Avenue to the Rob Roy. It took him half an hour. When he arrived there, it was a quarter past seven, and he was almost sober.

"See 'ere," he said to Johnnie aggressively. "I got to call my girl. I said I would yesterday and I went and forgot." It all came back to him. He felt he had let Freda down.

When he returned to Johnnie five minutes later, he said, "No good. She's fixed up. I'm seein' 'er tomorrow." And with the air of one settling down for the evening, he edged his way through the huddle to buy them both a pint.

VII

"Matt darling," Freda said. It was amusing, she thought, how her manner of speech changed when she was with Matthew and not with Derek. Listen to her now. "Matt darling, we aren't going to the Curzon are we, to see that Italian film?" Matthew's car was wedged between the red buses at Hyde Park Corner.

"Yes," he answered her distractedly. "I thought you wanted to." He was not giving her his whole attention. "I knew it. Woman driver." He hooted angrily. "Silly bitch. Did you see what she did?"

"I've seen it," Freda said. "The film I mean." She wondered if it would occur to Matthew that this was the foreign film she had seen with Derek. But the incident, which was important to her, had completely gone out of Matthew's head.

"What a bore," said Matthew. "Here we go. It's too late to change now, my love," he said, returning his thoughts to Freda. "And anyway, you came in on the party rather late, didn't you?"

"I don't mind," said Freda quickly. "I'd like to see it again. It's a good film."

In the narrow foyer of the cinema Eleanor Waters and Bob Graham were waiting for them.

"We've got the tickets," said Eleanor. Then she saw Freda and looked faintly displeased. She had been running after Matthew for a long time, not so much because she liked him, but because she had a delightful vision of herself as a doctor's wife. She was a member of a once noble and rich Irish family, now removed with some remnants of the noble Irish furniture, to a semi-detached villa in Highgate. She studied pharmacy at the Polytechnic, because she hadn't been quite clever enough to do science. She had pale red hair and a vapid, doll-like face, and a high voice which one expected at any moment to squeak 'Mama'. Bob Graham was her Matthew-substitute, her defence against that world of Polytechnic women students who thought it despicable not to have a 'steady'.

He studied pharmacy too, wore a duffle coat and longed to be accepted as an intellectual. He and Matthew had been born in the same Northern town and had attended the same kindergarten. Both students in London, they had begun a sporadic friendship that had previously found expression tipping shells out of little bags and counting them at Miss Crutchett's in Harrogate. Freda could not understand Matthew's friendship with someone so completely his intellectual antithesis.

"Hallo, Eleanor; hallo, Bob," she said. "I've gate-crashed I'm afraid." She smiled.

"Delighted to see you," said Bob warmly. He was rather fond of Freda. He considered her both attractive and superior and thought Matthew was a lucky chap.

"Hallo, Freda," said Eleanor, quickly masking the look of displeasure, because well-bred people never show what they feel.

"It's a good film," said Freda. "I saw it last week."

"I can't think why on earth you want to see it twice," said Eleanor irritably. She was most upset at not having the chance to sit by Matthew and whisper intelligent things to him during the evening.

"I think this sort of film can bear any amount of seeing," said Freda.

"Oh quite," Bob agreed eagerly.

All through the film, however, Freda was reminded of Derek. Her reactions to it were entirely in remembering what he had said, what she had said, and how he had looked. She visualized his profile—although it might have been his profile at the concert, for the two had become interchangeable in her memory by now. It was almost a shock when Matthew took her hand to hold it, and she looked to see *his* profile, which was aquiline and dark, and certainly not wide-eyed, and beyond that Eleanor's small unbearably neat head, and Bob's, which was so undistinguished it might have belonged to anybody.

"Chocolate?" asked Bob, cracking a bar into squares, and trying without success not to rustle the paper. Freda refused. She loathed eating in the cinema. But Matthew munched happily, and Eleanor nibbled like a mouse. Crunch, crunch, went their combined teeth. How irritating they all are, thought Freda, and she longed for Derek. But it was only until tomorrow after all.

The film ended. The word *Fine* appeared, infinitesimal in the centre of the screen, and grew suddenly large, rushing towards them until it filled the celluloid frame. At the same time, the curtains began to close, and blue lights shone on their satiny surface.

"Terrific film," said Matthew. "Do you want to stay for the rest of the programme?"

"Oh no," said Eleanor. "Documentaries are always dreary. It bores me to tears to see Welsh coal-miners swinging their lamps, and singing as they come out of the pits."

"Come on, Bob. Shift. We're not staying."

Bob stood up and began a stumbling exodus over the feet and umbrellas, knocking against the knees of the rest of the row.

Outside, when Eleanor was back from powdering her nose in the ladies' room, Matthew said, "How about a sandwich at the Rob Roy? It doesn't close for half an hour."

"Do I know the Rob Roy?" queried Eleanor in her piping voice.

"It's a famous place," said Matthew, "and lots of fun. Isn't it, Freda?"

"Yes," she nodded. "I'd love to go there. It's been ages."

"Hop in." Matthew unlocked his car.

When they arrived the pub was crowded, almost completely full. Only Davy, by virtue of his thinness, could move easily, and he was generally behind the bar. Eleanor's small mouth contracted until it was the size of a button. London pubs were always a bit common. It was so different in the country (she liked a nice mellow beamy country pub), or in Cambridge where you were sure of nice people. She had once had a boy friend in Cambridge. But all these men . . . she looked round disparagingly, then caught Matthew's eye and assumed a smile. Matthew was enjoying it immensely.

Their little party of four, encumbered by Bob's duffle coat which made twice of him in bulk, managed to edge a few feet from the door.

"Well, what's it to be?" asked Matthew. "Beer, and sandwiches, I suppose?"

Eleanor drank beer because it was the right 'student' thing to do, and besides, it was sporting. "A lager for me," she said.

"Anything but cheese sandwiches," said Freda. She was standing not more than two yards from where Derek was sitting, but he was quite hidden from sight. She saw a sailor's hat and her heart soared into her throat, but when the wearer turned round from the bar he had red hair and a red face and was thirty at least.

There were few women in the Rob Roy besides Freda and Eleanor. A soldier had his girl with him, and in one corner sat a middle-aged woman wearing glasses and a grey suit and a neat pink blouse done up to the throat, but she was tipsy in spite of these outward signs of respectability. She whispered and giggled to the man at her side, and he was embarrassed, and kept glancing round to see if her remarks were audible.

But otherwise there were only men. Soldiers, sailors, art students and artisans, men about town, and men around town, and alone, in a magic circle, a policeman in plain clothes, pipe in one hand and beer in the other.

"This is a queer pub, isn't it?" said Bob, who had been watching a pale-faced American eyeing a pink young guardsman for some moments. He said it bravely, as an intellectual should, knowing no boundaries.

"Students come here as well," said Matthew, arriving back with the sandwiches and overhearing. "And theatre people. It's got an historical reputation. Anyone who's anyone's been here. Bit of both, I'd say."

"How hateful," said Eleanor, drawing into herself almost visibly, like the folding up of a snail's horns before the final retirement into its shell. It seemed to Freda that like some strange little animal, or metal affected by temperatures, Eleanor expanded or contracted according to her mood and the environment. When she found things unpleasant or distasteful she seemed to grow smaller, her eyes, her mouth, her whole body.

Matthew tapped her on the arm.

"Freda, isn't that your sailor friend?"

"Where?" She spun round. She saw Johnnie. "No," she began, "that's not . . ." Then her eye fell on Derek. He was roaring with laughter. He had his hand on Johnnie's sleeve. Someone spoke to him from behind, and Derek dropped back. He was obviously with another friend. Into view wormed a little man with a paunch and a bald head.

"We won't risk repeating last night," said the little man, as they passed within an inch of Freda.

"Isn't it?" persisted Matthew. "Isn't that the one?"

"Yes," nodded Freda, "it is."

She wanted to call out, to attract attention, but she said nothing. A fourth man joined them, coming up the narrow stairs from the lavatory. He struggled into his overcoat, and Derek helped him. He was a little younger than the bald man, and as well dressed, but his face was flaccid and soft round the mouth, almost as if he didn't shave.

"It makes me quite sick," Bob murmured, watching them. This really wasn't the place to bring the girls.

The four men disappeared through the swing door into the street.

"I'm going to see," said Freda urgently. "Wait for me, Matt." She pushed through the surrounding people and looked along the pavement. Derek and his three companions were climbing into a large shiny car. She went back into the noisy saloon.

"I don't like it here," Eleanor was saying, her slightly protruding teeth biting delicately into her lower lip.

'As if some bee had stung it newly' thought Freda. The flesh bulged underneath the teeth like a little French water-grape.

"I hate perverts." She spoke to Freda. "That common sailor wasn't really your friend, was he? I mean . . ." her voice tailed off.

"Oh, don't be such a disgusting snob," Freda snapped. "Yes, he is my friend." He's my lover, she wanted to say. Now swallow that.

"He's having high jinks with his boy friend, now," said Matthew. "You've lost him to one of superior charm. It must have been the pot belly that tipped the scales."

Freda chose to argue with Eleanor. Her shock and misery found expression in attacking Eleanor, who was pouting and looking fastidious.

"All you can think about," she snapped, "is whether or not a person is 'common'. We obviously choose our friends for different reasons, Eleanor, but I can assure you that that sailor is worth twenty of you, in both intelligence and charm. I'd rather spend an afternoon in the company of a worth-while working-class boy than a year with a dull prim prig." Even as she spoke, Freda knew that this was a side-issue, that the real argument was not Derek's class, but his behaviour. He had been in a queer pub, with a couple of elderly homosexuals, and had left with them, and he was drunk. "Your class consciousness makes me sick," she said, her voice raised. "I prefer to make my judgements on individual merit and character."

"It's quite obvious you've been teaching in East London too long," said Eleanor. "For goodness' sake, Matthew, get some sense into her." She thought it rather astute to appeal to Matthew.

"She's a bit touchy about her sailor," said Matthew. "It's no good quarrelling, and we've finished our sandwiches, so let's go."

They waited while he unlocked the car.

"If I drop you two at the Underground," asked Matthew, "will you be able to find your way home? Highgate is so far, and I want to talk to Freda."

"Perfectly," said Eleanor. "That's quite all right, Matthew. We don't mind a bit, do we, Bob?" She thought this was the very moment to appear equable and sweet.

Back at Bannerton Gardens Matthew accompanied Freda to her flat.

"No coffee," he said, as she opened the front door. He sank down in a chair. "Freda, I'm not blind. What's up? Are you having some sort of affair?"

"Not some sort. An affair." She was strained emotionally to her capacity. She couldn't have pretended or lied or evaded, and she didn't want to.

"You saw he went off with a couple of queers?"

"I saw him go *out* with them. Yes."

"You're not seeing him any more, then?"

"He had asked me out this evening, but I couldn't go."

"So you allow your lovers substitutes? I should have imagined you would be more concerned."

"I am concerned. I'm jealous, I'm upset." She was almost

crying. "But it's my business, and I don't want a cross-examination. I'm tired, Matt, and I should like to go to bed."

"Very well." He stood up. "I wish you lots of amusing evenings with your sailor, when he manages to find time off from his more lucrative acquaintances. I take it *you* don't pay a stud fee?"

He went out and slammed the door.

That's it, thought Freda. Oh, Derek.

She began to cry.

VIII

"Thanks," said Derek. "You can drop me off anywhere along here."

They were driving down Oxford Street in Paul's smart Buick, with its plastic and chromium trimmings and every obtainable gadget. Paul had demonstrated them all with insistent pride, and Johnnie and Derek were accordingly full of admiration and awe.

"Sure you won't come back for a drink?" asked Rupert, turning his head towards the back seat.

"Quite sure, thanks. I'm not riskin' sleepin' till one tomorrow."

"'E's seein' 'is party," explained Johnnie drily. 'Party' was the naval expression for 'girl'.

"Oh, that explains it then. Be good, Smudge. Don't do anything I wouldn't do."

"That leaves me precious little, don't it."

These insinuating banalities exchanged, Paul, who had been driving more and more slowly, applied the brakes, and the car pulled up.

"Ring me any time you're at a loose end, Smudge."

"Thanks, I will." He opened the door and jumped out. "Be seein' you around, Johnnie." He closed the door, and walked off along the empty pavement. It was less than ten-thirty, but already this main thoroughfare was practically deserted. A few small shops had lighted window displays, but the big stores were all in darkness, iron gates across the entrance-ways. Upstairs in a stock-room a burglar alarm was ringing, but no one seemed likely to pay any attention to it. Paul's car, which had turned, drove past him and hooted a salutation, and Derek waved gaily in response. It wouldn't have hurt the old beefer to drive him a bit nearer home. Still, Paul hadn't got anything out of *him*. There was justice in that. And, thank God, tonight he wasn't too late for the tubes. The complete episode of the last two days was fast fading from Derek's memory. So many things happened ashore he couldn't remember them all, and he lived in the present and occasionally in the very near future, but never in the past. Somewhere on a piece of scrap paper he had Paul's telephone number, and he supposed he might use it one day, when he had nothing to do, or was broke, or was bored.

Freda had spent a restless and miserable night. How could he, how could he? she asked herself over and over again. That horrid, fat old man. She spared herself no unpleasant detail. She had always been so tolerant of inversion in others, but *not* Derek. He was young and male and normal. And after *her*. Oh, how could he?

She had not fallen asleep until the early morning, and woken only a few moments before Derek arrived. She was still in her dressing-gown, and her eyes were puffed, and she had worked herself up into a state of hysterical jealousy and distrust.

Derek appeared gay and spruce and affectionate. He had slept soundly, and was delighted to see her again. He felt no guilt for his absence the last two days, and was completely astonished at her intemperate onslaught. He took her hands in his, and she tore them away.

"Don't touch me."

He threw his cap on to the unmade divan and waited, astounded.

"I saw you last night, so you don't have to pretend."

"Pretend what?" He was genuinely bewildered. He hadn't even been particularly tight, so it couldn't have been that. Women were unpredictable. Who'd have thought he'd get a welcome like this?

"I saw you at the Rob Roy." Freda began to cry. "Give me a handkerchief, please, Derek."

He gave her the one that was tucked inside his jumper, and she blew her nose.

"Well, what's that to cry about? You didn't think I was teetotal, did you?" He tried to behave lightly, but he was at a loss, and felt uncomfortable, not for himself but for her, because raw expression of emotion struck him as despicable.

"I saw you go off with those men," she sobbed. "I saw you."

"So what?" Derek was suddenly angry. "I can go where I please with who I please I suppose. Just because I'm not with you I don't 'ave to stay 'ome, do I?" She was like all women, trying to keep watch on your movements. All the bloody same. He was aware of his disappointment.

She was frightened by his anger, but she went on, "You'll obviously go to bed with anyone. I thought it meant something to you with me, but the minute I'm not there you go off with horrible old men, not even another girl. I thought you . . . I thought I . . ."

"You shouldn't leap to bloody conclusions," Derek shouted at her. "If you must know, I left 'em at half-past ten, and what's more I've known 'em for years." He felt the exaggeration was justified, and besides, having said it, he believed it.

"Where were you Friday then?" wept Freda, shattered now that her theory was unfounded, not really sure that Derek was telling the truth, but wanting desperately to accept what he said. "Why were you with those men? Men like that don't want boys like you, unless . . ."

He curbed his annoyance. He hated rows, and his own burst of temper was over as quickly as it had begun.

"Listen to me." He held her arms hard. "Men like that like to be with matelots, even if we don't give 'em what they're after. Our uniforms do for us what a sexy dress does for a girl. True? And we're lighthearted, and don't mind a joke or two, and we get free cigarettes and drinks. That's sailors, Freda, and it's no good your tryin' to make out we're any different. First thing we does when we comes on leave, is to get lashed up for an evenin'. But you know quite well that I don't want another girl 'cept you, or a man neither, so don't forget it."

"But what about Friday?" She couldn't prevent herself from nagging. She had to get it all cleared up.

"I forgot. I meant to 'phone, honest. But I met my oppo, and we 'ad a few, and I clean forgot." Freda wasn't crying now. She gave him back his handkerchief.

"Here's your handkerchief. How could you forget, Derek? You were seeing *me*."

He shrugged slightly.

"I just did. I'm sorry, Freda. I said so once. It just 'appened. But I rang Saturday, didn't I? And I'd thought of you all the time up to seein' Johnnie. Then I forgot."

He supposed he shouldn't have forgotten, but women were so unreasonable. Anyway, he was here now, wasn't he? He put his arms round her and hugged her close.

"Derek, I'm sorry." He thought she was about to cry again. "It's only because I did want to see you so much. I didn't mean to nag."

"I know, I know." He kissed her gently, rocking her in his arms. "It's no good cryin' over what's done with, is it?"

There was a whole day ahead, and he almost loved her now. His irritation at her possessiveness was quite gone.

"I must have some coffee. I've had no breakfast."

"I'll do that. You get yourself dressed."

"Derek, why are you so nice to me? I don't deserve it after all the things I've thought about you."

He went into the kitchenette, and she dressed quickly and made the bed.

"I got an idea," said Derek, as they drank their coffee, sitting together in the big armchair. "How'd you like to come down to Portsmouth and 'ave a look round?"

He wanted to make up for any disappointments he had given her. He didn't feel he'd done anything wrong, but she thought he had, so he'd make amends.

"Oh, I'd love it. I'll pretend I'm ill, at school. Oh, Derek, how lovely. How angelic."

"But you mus'n't wear anythin' too dressed up." He was suddenly afraid she'd come looking like she did the night at the concert. His first thought had been to show her off, but he didn't want to make a laughing stock of himself.

"I won't. I promise. Something very ordinary. But nice, of course." She didn't want to offend him. "When shall we go?"

"Tomorrow, if you like."

"Oh yes, tomorrow." Life was wonderful after all. Another entire day. "I'll ring up school first thing, and say I'm sick."

"That's right. You do that." He was crazy about her. He'd never met a girl like her. The way she spoke was lovely. "What we goin' to do today? You got any plans?" Hadn't she always planned everything?

Freda hadn't, but she made some. It was going to be a perfect day, after such a horrible beginning. They went to Kensington Gardens, sauntered along the Broad Walk, watched the small white sails puffing across the Round Pond, looked at Peter Pan, and touched the bronze, it was so smooth.

They ate their lunch out of doors in the sunshine. Children ran over to them, and talked to them, saying idiotic but enchanting things. They fed the birds. They might have been any young lovers idling away the delightful afternoon. They walked again. The bandstand looked like a piece of icing confectionery, it was so ornate and colourful, and Freda pointed it out to Derek who thought it the most original idea he had ever heard.

They hired a boat, and Freda lay back and closed her eyes and when she opened them she saw Derek, handsome and sunburned and fair, rowing with pleasureable ease, and listened while he told her boastfully of his success at naval regattas.

"Derek?" She knew there was something she had intended to say. "You know Matthew, the boy we saw in the restaurant? It's all finished." She tried to use an expression that Derek would use himself. "We're through."

He rested on the oars, immediately wary.

" 'Cause of me?"

"No. It was bound to happen sooner or later. This just precipitated it."

"I wouldn't like it to be 'cause of me," he persisted.

At that moment he would have left her for ever. He was terrified of responsibility. He had taken on no responsibility his whole life, at school or anywhere. Other boys, less able than he, had been captains and monitors, but not Derek. He liked to be free. He'd given up Maureen because she clung to him. *She'd* given up other blokes through him, she said so that day in the Caff. He had made only one real decision in his life and that was to go wherever the navy sent him, and to abide, more or less, by its regulations. But that responsibility was merely a way of shrugging off greater ones that civilian life was bound to inflict.

Freda sensed his unrest, and realized she had said the wrong thing. His lack of ease brought back to her his thoughtless behaviour the last two days. He didn't 'phone me, she thought, because unconsciously he was afraid of being tied down. He is afraid now I'll become possessive about him, simply because I no longer have Matthew.

She was rather pleased at her analysis and deliberately changed the subject, and the tension between them slackened. She smiled at him, and he smiled back. They nearly bumped into a duck that was making a determined course down midstream, and in a moment their happiness was restored.

When their hour in the boat was up, they sat by the water and ate ice-creams, which were sticky and melting, and ran down their fingers as fast as they licked. Then they walked back to Bannerton Gardens hand in hand, discretion thrown to the winds.

"I don't care if we do meet her," said Freda defiantly. But Mrs. Gibson-Brown had gone to her sister's for the day.

"The gods are with us, aren't they?" smiled Freda, as they reached the flat safely.

Just imagine Maureen Lacey saying a thing like that.

Derek kissed her slowly, deliberately. He had spent her sort of day and he felt they had never been closer. He hoped she wouldn't spoil it now by not letting him stay.

"Freda?" he said, holding her a little away from him. "It's early to go now. Let me stay with you all night?"

He kissed her again with all the persuasive passion he could summon up. It was funny how, at times like these, he could think in so detached a way of how to handle a situation and decide the best line of approach, while still continuing to make love with a virtuosity which was not mechanical. He seemed able to exist on the mental and physical plane simultaneously, his mind and body completely separate, yet both functioning at their maximum.

What shall I say? thought Freda. She had never before found him so attractive. Why say no? If she sent him away would he bother to come back, to ring her up again? Was she kidding herself that his interest was more than a physical one? If he left her because she wouldn't let him stay the night then she had misjudged their relationship.

"Let me stay?" said Derek persistently.

She shook her head. "No, Derek," she said. "Don't think it's because I don't want to say yes, I do, but . . ."

"But?" His arms didn't relax their pressure, but the disappointment was evident in his face.

She turned her head away and rested it against his shoulder. She knew that if she looked at him there would be no decision for her to make.

"Derek, not this time." A suspicion had come into her mind. Keep him wanting, she told herself, and he'll go off and find someone else. But no, that was unlikely, for their situation was sufficiently unusual not to be easily replaced. She just wanted more time to be sure of herself, not of him.

"Okay," said Derek. "If that's 'ow you feel." He let her go. "It's ten, anyway. I'd better be pushin' off."

"You understand?" she said. "You do understand, don't you?"

He masked his disappointment, but he didn't smile.

"Oh sure, I understand." He kissed her again fiercely and his own feelings see-sawed. "Of course I understand."

"It's still all right about tomorrow, isn't it?" There was a note of anxiety in her voice.

"Yeah, I'll come round and pick you up tennish." He took up his hat. "Goodnight, Freda," he said again from the door. "It's been a good day, anyhow."

He took a train to Victoria and walked moodily to an all-night coffee stall, lit by an out-moded, spitting gas-jet.

"Cup of coffee," he said to the man.

"You look cheesed off, Jack," volunteered the attendant, turning the tap on the urn. "Sugar?"

Derek took the bowl from him, carefully avoiding the sugar

which had become brown and solidified from contact with wet teaspoons.

"What's up then?" asked the man, inviting Derek's confidence.

"There's only two things what ever bother a matelot," said Derek, stirring his coffee.

"Don't tell me," interrupted the man.

"Right first time," said Derek. He stayed talking and drinking free coffees until the stall closed down.

The Third Week

I

Mrs. Smith made no comment on her son's nocturnal absence, although she was quite certain she had heard him unlatch the door just before the clock struck seven. He had enjoyed the long walk from Victoria. It was a lovely cool dawn that promised a warm day, and it was very quiet in these huddled back streets. Every footfall, every sound of a milk bottle clinking on a step or a front door slamming was detached and clear. Indoors, Derek felt refreshed and slightly guilty, as one does when the rest of the household still sleeps. He just had time for a quick shave before his mother came downstairs and began to cook the breakfast.

"Your mate come round last night," she said to him. "So I told 'im it wasn't no good 'angin' about waitin' for *you*."

"Johnnie?" he asked, surprised.

"I don't know 'is name," said Mrs. Smith. She was being slightly acid. " 'E don't tell me that. All 'e says is, 'Is Derek Smith in?' and when I say no, off 'e goes to the nearest public 'ouse." Mrs. Smith had married a seaman. She had no illusions.

"Well, I'm goin' out again soon," Derek informed her shortly. "So if 'e wants to see me, 'e'll 'ave to come back quick. I'm goin' down to Pompey."

"I should 'ave thought you'd 'ave 'ad enough of it to last you a week or two," retorted Mrs. Smith. The old girl was certainly a bit sharp this morning.

During breakfast Joan talked excitedly about her fifteenth birthday which was on Wednesday.

"You'll be 'ere for my party, won't you, Derry?" she said persuasively. "I'm only 'avin' a few of the girls in for tea." She giggled. "I'm goin' dancin' in the evenin', special, with Ronnie Mendicott."

"Dunno what you see in 'im," growled Derek. He didn't want to be tied down to tea on Wednesday.

"You will come, won't you?"

"Yeah," he promised sacrificially. "I'll be there. Mum," he said, "I'll just give me shoes a rub up, and I'll be off."

"I suppose we'll next 'ave the pleasure of seein' you on Wednesday," said Mrs. Smith, "if you can make it."

After nearly a whole year away foreign, she thought, he can't stay home for more than a few hours. Still, the young don't want to hang around all day, they like a bit of larking about. But she wished he wasn't so secretive, all the same. She knew he could look after himself, but it was worrying not knowing where he was, who he'd picked up with.

" 'Bye, all," came his cheerful voice from the hallway. He had evidently rubbed up his shoes. The door slammed.

II

Freda was looking forward to this day at Portsmouth tremendously. Since she had sent him away last night she felt more self-respect, and her urge to educate Derek had returned. Portsmouth was just the place for them to go, because he knew the town geographically, but he wouldn't know the history.

She had hurriedly checked the history of the town in the encyclopaedia, what she called 'footnote' history, and she hoped his interest would be awakened, and they could go and look at the house where Dickens was born. With luck they might even have time to go across to Hayling Island to see the church with its fifteenth-century doorway and its twelfth-century font. She had been there when she was quite small, and in Hayling graveyard was the epitaph:

> Ye Virgins fair, your fading charms survey,
> She was whate'er your tender hearts can say,
> Let opening roses, drooping lilies tell,
> Like these she bloomed, and ah! like these she fell.

Freda often put that in autograph albums when the girls thrust those pink and blue pages at her across the desk. One had to be didactic to the virgins fair of Jubilee Road. She thought this verse was perfect, because it was sufficiently remote from contemporary speech, and yet it was perfectly clear in meaning, and terribly apposite.

But in spite of my plans for educational visits to educational places, she thought, smiling to herself, I'll quite probably end up in Southsea Funfair. I think I might even prefer to end up in Southsea Funfair. It was enticing to think of a ride with Derek on the Dodgems, or clinging to him while they swung aloft on the Bigwheel.

This is Derek's day, not mine, she decided, so I won't try to influence him at all. She knew she had an instinct to dominate, which was why she liked teaching, but she longed to be dominated by Derek because in her heart she believed she was in the superior position.

Derek arrived at a quarter to ten, and was relieved to see she was wearing a cotton frock, for in spite of her promise he had had fears of something embarrassingly posh.

"It's going to be lovely weather again," she said. "How lucky we are." She had her sunglasses in her handbag. "Shall I take my camera?"

"No. What for?"

"To take some snaps of *you*."

He was gratified. "All right then. Ready? If we leave now there's a train that will get us there nice for opening time."

Freda looked at him swiftly to see if this was a joke, but he couldn't have appeared more serious. The train would get them there nice for opening time. What could be more favourable than that?

"Yes, I'm ready." She had been ready since nine. She had two bars of chocolate to eat on the train in case they were hungry, and a cardigan to wear in case it became cold in the evening.

"Let's get weavin' then." He kissed her quickly and affectionately, and squeezed her hand before they locked the front door and ran down the stairs past Mrs. Gibson-Brown's flat and out into the sunshine.

At Waterloo, for the first time in her life, Freda was conscious of the number of sailors everywhere. Their white caps caught the eye at the ticket offices and bookstalls, dotted along the platforms.

"There's always matelots 'ere," said Derek when she commented. "Comin' and goin'. Never known it not."

They waited hand in hand at the barrier for the Portsmouth train. Freda was in the mood for an excursion. Music was playing through a loud-speaker, and the sunshine filtered dustily into the station.

"I believe that's my oppo down there," said Derek suddenly, when they were on the platform. "There, just gettin' into that carriage." He craned his head to see over the shoulder of the man in front. "My life if it ain't Johnnie." He raced ahead, impatient and excited. "I'm just goin' to see, Freda," he shouted back to her. "Don't kid me 'e's got a double."

In a moment he was back again, Johnnie Cooper hanging sheepishly in the rear.

"It was 'im," called out Derek. "What'd I tell you? My Mum told 'im I was goin' to Pompey, and 'e thought 'e'd risk findin' me." He was transparently delighted. He adored Johnnie. Freda hid her disappointment and Derek introduced them both with undisguised pride.

"My old woman's in 'ospital," explained Johnnie, who sensed an explanation was in order, "and me Dad's gone and gone off to me Uncle's up Ealin' way. I was on me own and so bloomin' chokka I thought I'd go off me nut. So I went round to Smudge's place for a bit of company."

There was something about Johnnie's expression that implied he had joined them for the day. He won't stay with us all the time, thought Freda. Surely Derek won't let him.

" 'Ope you don't mind," Johnnie said to Freda.

"Of course not." She recovered from her initial disappointment, and prepared to enjoy Johnnie's presence. There seemed little alternative. And anyway, she felt rather sorry for him.

There is an air of restlessness about Portsmouth. It seems to exist solely for the navy and the navy is always changing. Like

Aldershot or any barrack town, it has a shifting population with no roots, and this restlessness affects everybody. Derek, straight from his united family breakfast table, was possessed of a wild longing to go to sea again, at once. Johnnie found the exciting instability more fitting for his humour, more his element than his disrupted home. Even Freda, standing on the harbour platform built out over the sea to facilitate loading on to the Isle of Wight Ferry, was made to feel nostalgic for the security of her childhood by the unsettled atmosphere. It was the sight of the fresh-faced boys waiting to go on leave, sitting on their cases, lolling against the walls of the refreshment bar, and their identical counterparts jumping out of the compartments, naïvely eager to get to the pubs or report to their ships, that affected her, they all seemed so defenceless.

It was windy on the high platform, even on such a warm day. Collars flapped in the wind and Freda straightened Derek's for him, finding pleasure in the feel of the hard muscle of his shoulder underneath. His uniform was becoming more and more romantic to her.

"It just evolved," he had told her last night, when she had been surprised at his use of the word. "No one thought it up like. The collars was to stop the tar comin' off pigtails and messin' up the uniform underneath."

She thought of that now, as the collar blew up again the moment she let it go, covering the back of his neck.

"That's the masts of the *Victory* over there," Johnnie told her, pointing.

Freda breathed in the acrid tang of the seaweed and looked at the three masts, just showing in the distance.

"Come and see the Mudlarks," said Derek—for there were still ten minutes to go before opening time.

He took her hand and led her out of the main entrance to the concrete road running between the station and the front, carried on piles over the shallow water thick with dirt and refuse.

"Kids," he said. "Look." He flipped a penny into the air and it fell, spinning into the mud below. Two or three urchins, their clothes soaked, ran shouting to search for it, found it, and looked up for more.

"They're always there," said Derek. "Mudlarks."

He felt he had shown her the sights, and he was thirsty.

"There's only one thing what redeems this flamin' town," said Johnnie, as they walked along, past the dockyard gates, "and that's there're more pubs per square mile than anywhere else in the world."

Derek laughed happily. It wasn't half good being back in old Pompey with Johnnie. Fleetingly he wished Freda wasn't with them, but when he looked at her, and saw she was laughing too, with her hair and skirt blowing in the wind, he was glad after all, and having her with him added to his happiness.

"Where shall we go?" asked Johnnie, with the air of one who has so many delicious things to choose from that the choice is impossibly hard.

"Compasses?"

"Compasses."

"I bet you didn't know," said Derek to Freda, "that in the old days all the pubs 'ad straw on the floor so no one'd 'ear when a drunk sailor dropped 'is money, and the landlord swiped it."

"I didn't know," said Freda, pleased that she didn't know, and amused at all the useless information Derek accumulated.

"Never thought I'd be one up on a teacher." He pressed her arm.

"Go on," said Johnnie, aghast. "You ain't a teacher, are yer?"

Freda nodded, smiling. "I teach Derek's sister."

"What you doin' with 'er?" asked Johnnie more dubiously, as he and Derek stood in the scrum round the Compasses' familiar bar. "A teacher! Don't tell me she does yer a turn?"

"Oh shu' up," said Derek, suddenly disgusted. "It's not like that." But he couldn't resist adding with a grin. "But she does, all the same."

"Does she now." Johnnie turned to have another look at Freda, who was sitting on a wooden bench waiting for her drink. It's just like a university pub, she was thinking. There it's all students. Here it's all sailors. Her attention was suddenly riveted to the hideous old woman who was sidling into the bar. She was wearing a red silk dress cut very low, and the skin at the top of her breasts was a mass of tiny creases. Her hair looked as if it hadn't been washed for months. It hung over her forehead in a greasy peek-a-boo bang.

"That's Pompey Minnie," said Derek, handing Freda a gin and lime—he was going to do things properly, today. "What you think of 'er?"

"Horrible," said Freda. She sipped the gin which she hated.

Derek suddenly recalled the day he had last come ashore, and was standing here in the Compasses with Fauntleroy.

"She's like somethin' painted by that artist bloke," he said. "The one what painted women like 'er. A Frog, a cripple I think 'e was."

"Toulouse-Lautrec?" Freda was captivated by Derek's sudden bursts of knowledge. Whoever would have imagined he'd have heard of Lautrec?

"Yeah, that's the one," he said.

Of course, thought Freda, the very painter who *would* appeal to him. The scenes of lurid night life would strike an immediate chord with his own experiences. She wondered if he knew the one of the two people in bed. And how clever of him to see the likeness to Pompey Minnie. She was about to say something more, when she realized that Derek was listening enthralled to a story being told by a weasel-faced little sailor with uneven teeth.

"So I says to 'er, I says, 'You can put 'em on again, lass! That clears me,' I said."

There were roars of admiring laughter. Johnnie was uncontrollable.

"So what she say to that?" he gasped helplessly.

Freda had a prickly feeling. Will Derek talk about me like this, she thought, when I'm not here? She had somehow become the centre of a little group of sailors and they were eyeing her appreciatively. Derek suddenly claimed her. She was his girl, after all.

"'Ave another, Freda?"

She began to decline, but he took the glass from her.

"Nope! No arguin'. I want this to be a nice day for you. She ain't never been to Pompey before," he told the boys.

"It's a lousy dump," one of them said morosely. "Nothin' but slummy little 'ouses."

"Well, it wasn't planned, was it? It grew. And besides, there *are* some lovely houses, Adam houses, I know." As she spoke she knew how stupid and prudish she was being.

"Thought you ain't been 'ere before."

"Dunno about *Adam* 'ouses, but we could do with a few more *Eve* 'ouses, couldn't we?"

"I've read about it," said Freda. But her voice was lost in the raucous merriment.

She felt desperately that she couldn't find their level. She couldn't seem to talk naturally, only like a school teacher in front of a class. It was becoming a nightmare, alone in a pub, with Pompey Minnie and a bunch of obscene sailors.

"Derek," she said, determined to end it, as he gave her another gin and lime. "I wondered if we might go to Hayling Island?"

"'Aylin'?" he asked, astonished and unreceptive. "What the 'ell for?"

"There's an old church I'd like to see, and a famous gravestone."

"Famous gravestone?" chuckled weasel-face.

"Yes," said Freda defiantly. "A warning to women."

That struck home. She was with them. They were with her.

"Go on. Tell us!"

"I could give 'em a warnin' or two!"

"Let's 'ave it then."

"Ye virgins fair," began Freda.

She got no further. It was the funniest thing they had ever heard. They shouted, they held their sides, they leant against each other for support.

"Ye virgins," they managed to say at intervals. "Ye old English virgins." They elaborated on the joke till it was exhausted, and nothing was left to be said. Freda felt she would cry if they went on a moment more.

"Come on," said Johnnie. "Let's go over to the Star."

"Let's 'ave another one 'ere first," suggested weasel-face. "What's the 'urry?"

So they stayed and had another one and another one and another. Then Freda said, "I'm sorry, Derek, but I must have some fresh air. It hardly seems worth coming all this way to spend the whole day in a pub. We could have done that in London."

Derek looked at her blankly.

"Okay," he said, "but they'll be closed in another 'alf-hour. Just let's 'ave one more in the Star, then we'll go to 'Aylin', or wherever it is you want."

"Let's get goin' then," urged Johnnie, taking Freda's arm.

A group of them moved unsteadily to the door of the lavatory.

"We'll catch you up," called Derek over his shoulder.

Freda found herself in the street, weasel-face at her side.

"My name's Chalky White," he said. "What's yours?"

"Freda."

"Like an 'amburger, Freda?"

The sight of the hamburger stall was suddenly attractive. She realized she was hungry.

"I'd love one," she said gratefully. They joined the queue. This is my lunch, she thought, as she bit into the piece of protruding sausage meat that had already become lukewarm.

"Come on," Chalky said impatiently, "or we'll miss the others."

They hurried over to the Star, eating as they went. It was packed full of sailors. After the fresh air, the smell of beer, combined with the fatty taste of the hamburger which had stopped being delicious after the first few mouthfuls, made Freda feel slightly sick.

"They don't seem to be 'ere," announced Chalky, after a brief survey. "Reckon they must 'ave gone to the Victory, instead."

"No," answered Freda, "they said the Star. They just haven't arrived yet." They waited for a few moments on the pavement.

"They ain't comin'," said Chalky. "They've gone to the Victory on the way. We 'ates passin' a pub, you know."

"But he said the Star," insisted Freda. Yet if he's drunk, she thought, he's quite possibly forgotten and gone with the others. She began to hate the day and the sailors with their coarse jokes and their pointless drinking for the sake of drinking.

Chalky took Freda's arm and walked her swiftly down the narrow street, grey houses on one side of them, a bleak brick wall, apparently gateless, on the other. They turned into the Victory. That, too, was full of navy blue.

"Not 'ere," reported Chalky. "I reckon we'd better try the Eight Bells."

They set off again, and crossed into a main street. Every other shop seemed to display blazers and uniforms, and caps and badges.

"You wait 'ere," said Chalky, stopping outside the bow-fronted Eight Bells. "I'll just 'ave a quick dekko."

He disappeared into the pub, and as the door swung, so the noise eddied into the street. In a second or two he was with her again.

"They must be somewhere," he said, scratching the back of his head. " 'Ow about the Rose and Crown?"

"No," Freda said, furious and tired. "I'm not going to spend the day searching a succession of dreary pubs."

"What shall we do then?" He considered himself her escort, and was hurt by her tone.

"I don't care what *you* do. I'm going back to London by the next train."

Chalky gallantly took her to the station. He tried to hold her arm again, soothingly, and she shrugged him irritably away. The sun was brilliant, a green charabanc swept past them. A happy little girl let a shower of orange peel blow backwards from the window. The people inside were singing.

"I'll see you on to the platform," said Chalky amiably.

There, waiting for the London train, were the sailors going on leave. They might have been the same sailors that were there when she arrived two hours ago. It goes on and on and on, she thought, this endless succession. One was swigging a bottle of beer. His head was tipped back to get the last dregs, so that for a moment all that could be seen was his throat working contentedly. The train came in.

"I want a carriage without sailors," said Freda tartly. "I'm sick of sailors."

"Just 'cause we lost 'em, it's no need to talk like that," reproved Chalky, offended. "It's daft."

But nevertheless he helped her find an empty compartment, and then stood back awkwardly on the platform.

"Thank you, Chalky," said Freda, dismissing him. "And if you should happen to see Derek, you can tell him I've gone back to London."

"Okay," said Chalky. "Be seein' you." He walked away and crossed the line by the footbridge.

Within a few minutes two sailors came into Freda's carriage. She looked out of the window at the brightly coloured posters of seaside towns, each one with its sky and sea painted in clear untrammelled blues.

"Like a cigarette?" offered one of the sailors, producing the white packet with the navy-blue letters R.N. on it, that she associated with Derek. He winked at his mate.

"No thank you." She looked out of the window again. One thing I'm quite certain about, she told herself, as the wheels seemed to grip the lines for that split second before the train drew out, I've seen the last of Derek Smith. I never want to see him again.

III

"Where's Freda?" asked Derek, as soon as he was settled with his pint of black and tan in the saloon of the Star and Garter.

"She stopped with old Chalky for an 'amburger," informed someone. "She'll be along in a minute."

"I'd better go and 'ave a look," said Derek, conscience-stricken and full of remorse.

"Oh, come off it, Smudge. She's not a bleedin' kid."

"I know, but she come down 'ere with me. I got to look after 'er, 'aven't I?"

"Well, give 'er a chance to eat 'er flamin' 'amburger, mate."

Derek was about to answer in his own defence, when the door opened, and into the bar sauntered two pretty girls in coloured sundresses. Their shoulders were bare, and one of them had red hair. Derek had a weakness for red hair.

" 'Allo, Carrots," he said.

"None of the 'carrots', if you don't mind," retorted the girl with a Scots accent. Another point in her favour. Derek had once loved a nippie in Rosyth.

"Can I get you ladies a drink?" asked Jock Wilson, who recognized the accent as belonging to a 'townie' of his, Glasgow, to be exact.

The ladies were delighted. A moment's conversation and it became apparent they were at a loose end and going to Southsea that afternoon. By strange coincidence, Jock and Johnnie had set their hearts on going there as well, but the redhead seemed to have inclinations towards Derek, and gave him the most provocative glances, and lowered her sandy lashes, and flashed him several special smiles.

It was nearly ten minutes before Derek remembered Freda again. He was terribly upset.

"Didn't we say we was goin' to the Star?" he demanded sharply of Johnnie. "That's where she's gone. I'm goin' to 'ave a look."

He pelted across the street and into the Star and stared round. Fancy losing her like this. Anxiously he ran back to the Star and Garter.

"'As she turned up?" he asked.

"Nor Chalky," answered Johnnie, with an insinuating smirk.

"You lay off that lark," threatened Derek. But he was extremely worried. "What'll I do?" he said bleakly.

"Wait 'ere," suggested Jock, who had just made the delightful discovery that the redhead lived only three streets away from his own home. "She'll come over here for certain when she sees you're not in the Star."

Derek waited five minutes, pacing up and down.

"I'm goin' to do a quick round of the pubs," he announced shortly. "You blokes wait for me 'ere, see, and if she comes, tell 'er where I am."

He could have bashed his head against a wall, he was such a bloody fool. He seemed to be making a habit of letting her down when he didn't mean it. Now, if he *meant* to give a girl the go-by, she'd come rushing back for more, you could bet your life, and when for once he wanted to keep a girl, this was what happened. Talk about—— There was no word in his vocabulary to do justice to his behaviour.

He went back to the Star. He went on over to the George. He

turned left for the Eight Bells. He looked in on the Compasses again, but the only woman there was Minnie trying to embrace a flushed young rating. Eventually he returned to the Star and Garter.

"No luck," he said morosely to Johnnie. "Think I'll come to Southsea this afternoon. I ain't likely to find 'er now."

"Oh well," comforted Johnnie philosophically, "I dare say we can find you another party before the day's out."

But Derek wanted Freda. He tagged along sullenly behind the gay foursome which was walking towards Southsea. He snatched at the leaves of a privet hedge and tore them into little bits, leaving an emerald trail on the dusty pavement. When he saw an empty lemonade bottle he kicked it viciously, shattering the glass against the kerb-stone, so that the sun momentarily transfixed each splintered piece as if there had been a miniature explosion there in the gutter.

"Oh, come off it, for Christ's sake," said Jock. "The girl'll understand when you explain. It could've 'appened to anyone."

"Will she just," muttered Derek. "I've 'ad a dose of 'er understandin'."

They went to the Funfair, and Derek picked up the plainest girl he could find, made her pay for herself ("A sailor's pay ain't much, you know"), and when she offered him her red mouth in the twilight of the Ghost Ride, he stared stonily ahead. He dropped her again the moment it was opening time, and settled himself morosely in the nearest pub, where he stayed for an hour or so without speaking to anyone but the barman.

He could find another party, could he? Well, he didn't want another party, he wanted Freda. He loved Freda. He was sure he loved her. Fancy going and losing a girl like that. Pretty, and posh, and clever too.

By the time he caught the train back to London he had become quite sentimental, a way in which drinking seldom affected him.

He was determined to have a corner seat so that he could sleep in comfort, and as soon as he got to Smoke he was going to Freda's to see if she was back yet. But the train was packed full of day-excursion holiday makers, carrying china ornaments marked 'A present from Southsea', and empty picnic baskets and crumpled coats. By a stroke of luck he managed to find a corner seat and sat down with a sigh of relief. An old woman closed the window, and then fell asleep and began to snore, quietly but continuously. In the opposite corner a spooning couple held hands and stroked arms and gazed at each other. There were three over-excited, over-tired children.

The spooning depressed Derek and the snoring and the children got on his nerves. He sat tense for the first hour of the journey, and then lurched out of the compartment for a bit of peace and fresh air. As he staggered down the corridor he realized that his unsteadiness was not entirely due to the swaying of the train. He was, in fact, quite drunk, that delayed-action drunkenness that gradually seeps through the resistance of the habitual drinker. He unslung a window and leaned out, staring at the opposite tracks illuminated by the glow of the lighted corridor. As the train sped over points and crossings the lines would separate and join, then separate again, then group themselves into parallel lines of four and six, then back to two as the junction was passed. It was like watching the weaving of a gigantic cat's cradle, and his eyes began to ache.

As the train neared London it started to rain, and Derek was forced to close the window. He supposed he'd have to face the carriage again. He hoped those two had stopped mucking about, that was all. Christ, his head hurt.

He walked back along the corridor, thrown first to one side and then the other. One of the fractious children was blocking the way, and beyond him Derek could hear the grizzling of another.

" 'Scuse *me*," he said sarcastically to the child, and pushed past him into the next compartment. He steadied himself against the door and went to sit down.

A man was sitting in his seat. *His* seat.

" 'Ere," said Derek abruptly, "that's my seat you're in."

The man looked up from his newspaper, slightly annoyed, more by Derek's tone than his assertion.

"I think you've made a mistake," he said with restraint.

"Oh, no I 'aven't," said Derek. "You're the one what's made the mistake. Your mistake is sittin' in my seat." To his own surprise he followed this with an obscene word. He didn't really mean to, but on the mess-deck its use was commonplace. Then he hiccupped.

"Get out," ordered the man. "You're drunk."

Derek drew himself up as straight as he could.

"That's my seat you're sittin' in," he said slowly, "and that's my seat you're goin' to get out of."

"If you don't go I'll call the guard," the man retorted angrily.

Derek leaned forward and took hold of the lapels of the man's jacket, dragging him to his feet. Then still holding him by one lapel, he aimed a clumsy right at the man's jaw. The man avoided the blow, and Derek's fist shattered the glass of a sepia photograph of Chichester castle which was screwed to the panel above the seat. Glass splintered down on to the upholstery, and blood spurted from Derek's knuckles. He swore loudly. A woman in the opposite corner screamed even more loudly. The man grabbed Derek's right wrist. Derek flung his weight against the man, pinning him in the corner. Then his left fist crashed savagely into the side of the man's face, and split the cheek.

Almost immediately Derek's arms were gripped from behind and twisted up into the small of his back. He jerked back his head sharply, expecting to feel his skull in contact with the face of the person holding him. But there was no such contact. Instead a hard knee was thrust painfully into the middle of his spine.

"Take it easy, Jack," warned a voice. "I've done unarmed combat too."

Derek struggled, but it was no use. His arms were locked. The knee increased its pressure.

"Call the guard," demanded the man whose cheek Derek had split.

As the train swung through Clapham Junction the guard appeared and Derek's captor released him from his bone-snapping hold. By now Derek had sobered up. With a handkerchief round his knuckles, he listened glumly as the occupants of the compartment recounted his attack.

"I shall 'ave to report this when we arrives at Waterloo," said the guard, indicating the shattered glass of the picture. "Are you takin' up the matter with the police, sir?"

"I don't think so," said the man, tenderly feeling the cut on his face. "I'd be happy to help put this young thug behind bars, but my time is too important to waste with police court actions. I have to be in Glasgow tomorrow morning."

"You're not safe nowhere, nowadays," put in the woman opposite, determined not to be left out. "I just got over a nervous breakdown," she went on, "been stayin' with me sister down in Southsea. 'E's fair upset me, 'e 'as. If I 'ave another attack, 'oo's goin' to pay the doctor's bill, that's what I want to know? 'E come in 'ere like a . . ."

"Oh, shu' up," said Derek. "I didn't touch you, did I?"

The man who had held Derek spoke.

"The only person who has cause for complaint," he said, "is this gentleman who was attacked. And if he's not going to pursue the matter, the best thing to do is to forget the whole incident. I'm sure this young man realizes what a rotten spectacle he's made of himself, and a proper apology is all that seems to be necessary."

"I'm afraid not," said the guard heavily. "I shall 'ave to give 'im in charge for wilfully damagin' railway property. I sees too much of this sort of thing in my job. These blokes get away with it all the time, especially on this run. Not a day goes past without a winder gets smashed, or the seats get cut. We 'as to clamp down somewhere."

The woman who had suffered from a nervous breakdown was the only one ready to supply her name and address as a witness. The two men got down together.

"You should think yourself lucky, Jack, that you're not in a worse mess," said the one whose knowledge of unarmed combat had prevented Derek from further violence. "Next time don't mix your drinks."

Derek didn't answer. He felt utterly miserable. He stayed with the guard while the train emptied, then they walked down the long platform together.

"No monkey tricks now," said the guard, half-expecting Derek to make a run for it. He was a red-faced man in his middle-fifties, and he wasn't quite sure what he would do if Derek did decide to take to his heels. "We don't only carry our whistles for startin' off the train," he said impressively.

"Oh, put a sock in it. Blow your bleedin' whistle if you want," said Derek. He felt too sick and tired of the whole business to contemplate trying to escape.

A policeman was standing within a few yards of the barrier. He listened with a stony face to the guard's story, then he transferred the details into his own notebook with irritating slowness.

"You're comin' with me, my lad," he said to Derek. "You blokes'll never learn, will yer?"

From the R.T.O.'s office the constable telephoned for a police van, and they drove to the police station at Kennington Road, where Derek was formally charged with being drunk and disorderly, and with wilfully damaging railway property.

IV

He woke up at two in the morning hearing a clock strike, and with confused memories of his arrival at the police station. The white glazed bricks of the walls shone luminously in the light from the one window seven feet high. In the moonlight, which was bright, the bars looked flat and two-dimensional. Under his head was a hard pillow made of rough sacking and by the feel of it filled with straw. The mattress was supported on three trestle-balanced planks.

Jail, thought Derek. What a life. His hand was aching and bruised and he examined the knuckles ruminatively, trying to recollect the fight. Was that two or three it struck just then? How many more hours till morning? He sat up to look at his watch, to hold his arm at a better angle for the light, but his wrist was bare. Of course. He remembered now. They'd taken all his belongings when he got here before they pushed him into this hole. Not even a bleeding fag to ease up with. 'Struth, he said to himself, but without any real hostility, they don't even leave you a bleedin' fag. And then he fell asleep.

When he woke again it was morning, and a dark blue silhouette said, "Come on, look lively now," and he sat up, stiff from the unyielding straw bedding.

It was an elderly police constable.

" 'Ere's your breakfast," he told Derek. "Eat it quick and then you can 'ave a nice tidy up for His Honour." He put down a plate with two sausages on it that had grown cold on their way from the canteen, a thick mug of tea and a piece of bread and margarine cut diagonally as if it was a dainty sandwich at a vicarage tea.

"Not much of a breakfast," muttered Derek, glancing at it.

"Enough of that, lad," said the constable, offended. "It's more'n you deserve."

Derek was hungry and could have eaten twice as much. The meal finished, the constable returned, unlocked the door and marched Derek along to the washroom which was in the same barred area as the cells. He supervised the cold water ablutions and gave Derek a razor to shave with.

"You're goin' to look decent before you come up before His Honour," he said, as if Derek was his own particular property. He dropped all aitches except those.

"Anyone think I was gettin' spliced," said Derek, "the fuss you're makin'."

The impertinence was received in stony silence, and Derek was escorted, disgraced, back to his cell.

"You'll be fetched when it's time," said the constable, and the door closed behind him.

Derek sat on the edge of the bed and pondered gloomily on the situation. He saw alternatives and none was pleasant. He'd get time or he'd be fined, and if he hadn't got enough on him they would send for a naval escort and his leave would be docked. And if he had enough to pay, it would just about leave him skint. He might as well be in prison as be in London without money. In any case, he wouldn't be able to see Freda again. The only way he asserted himself over Freda was by paying for her, and he had the suspicion that if he was broke she'd insist on paying for them both. That idea was so humiliating it made his blood run cold. He couldn't help feeling obscurely that Freda had got him into this.

The cell door opened again.

"Come on, Jack," commanded the constable. "Your turn next and no disrespect, mind."

And Derek, his repartee completely deserting him, was taken from his cell and across the road to the police court. He waited in a gloomy passageway with an absurd collection of police constables, prostitutes, tramps and grey-faced gentlemen in crumpled blue-serge suits. Then his case was called and he entered the courtroom and mounted a low platform with a worn wooden rail in front of it.

The morning sun shone directly on to the magistrate, and he asked for the blinds to be drawn. The usher became busy with the thick cords and untwisted them from their brass hooks. Beige canvas slowly descended and lidded the windows. The green walls became shadowy.

The disturbance over and the magistrate settled again, Derek's case began. The constable read out particulars in a loud voice devoid of expression. Derek's gloom increased at every word.

"First offence?" asked the magistrate in a dry bored voice. He looked like a bird with hooded eyes, as if years of having the blinds down had adapted him to a life of semi-darkness.

"First offence, Your Honour," said the constable.

The magistrate turned his head the fraction of an inch towards Derek, for the first time intimating that this wasn't merely an academic dispute but that somewhere a human being entered into it.

"Have you anything to say?"

"I'd like to say I'm sorry, sir," said Derek meekly.

You'd be sorry too, he wanted to shout, if you'd lost your girl and cut your hand and spent the night in clink. You'd have felt like I did and had a drink over the odds, so there's no need to look at me like you was a bleeding saint.

"I'm going to fine you two pounds with thirty shillings costs. Are you able to pay that sum?"

"Yes, sir," answered Derek, his heart like lead. That left him ten bob to finish his leave with, and five days to go.

"It's difficult to expect hooligans like yourself to have any respect for public property and public services," said the magistrate, "but I should have thought you might have desisted from smashing up the railways when you were wearing the uniform of your Queen and country." The flat scorn in his voice made Derek uncomfortable. He was proud of being in the navy and loved it in spite of the things he sometimes said to the contrary. He hadn't let the navy down. It was a private thing to do with himself, getting drunk. You didn't stop having emotions just because you were in the Andrew.

"Next case," said the magistrate.

"Next case," called the usher.

As Derek left the courtroom he saw ascending the little platform in his stead an old man with uncut hair and untrimmed beard, a long woollen scarf wound round his neck and a Bible prominently under his arm. Poor old tub-thumper, Derek thought sympathetically. The morning had worn off his hard edges. Imagine being old and then had up for something you really believed in. It was a bloody shame.

He collected his cigarettes, his watch and his wallet, and paid his fine with grudging martyrdom, having been trodden underfoot by the law. Then he left the station and stood in the street just outside, wondering what to do.

No money, no Freda, and he didn't want to go home. He scarcely admitted to himself he felt ashamed. What would Mum say if she knew he'd spent the night in prison? It would upset her something dreadful. He suddenly thought he knew how deserters felt, loose on the world and nowhere to go, glad of friendship on any terms.

Blimey, he said to himself, I'm a proper misery this morning. He was fed up to the last degree. He had a sudden idea and went into the 'phone booth outside the police station and dialled Paul's number, but there was no reply. He visualized the telephone ringing on the highly polished half-table set in the crimson and white alcove in the hall. He slammed down the receiver and went out again into the grey Waterloo street.

What now? He walked swiftly until he came to the Thames embankment, which brought vividly into his mind the evening with Freda at the Festival Hall, and found a milk-bar with worn Festival décor of faded greys and yellows, a spidery abstract mural along one wall. He sat down wearily at a bamboo table as if the burden of life was unremitting.

"Tea," he said curtly, "and a couple of buns."

The buns were faded too, but he was still very hungry and he felt cheered when he had eaten them. Should he go back early from leave? Catch the navy saying no to a sucker! Or should he go down to the West End and get picked up, which would tide him over today and tonight too? In the end he decided to go home after all. It wouldn't hurt him to spend the last few days at home. In fact the prospect of undemanding evenings with his family, and food cooked for him lovingly by his mother, was as tempting as the desire to make love to Freda had been a day or so ago.

He paid for his buns and tea and walked back to the Underground and took a ticket for Mile End.

By the time he got there his guilty feelings with regard to his mother had reached such a peak, he spent some of his last few shillings on a tin of green paint to assuage them. He'd paint the front door for the old girl. That would make her happy. She'd been on about it as long as he could remember.

Jubilee Road was enjoying a lull of mid-morning quietness. The babies slept and the older children were at school.

"Mum," called out Derek, as he pushed open the front door.

She was in the kitchen, making Joan's birthday cake for the tea party tomorrow. Along the window-sill ten orange jellies were setting.

"That you, Derry?" She had made up her mind to speak to him. Busy for the happiness of one child had made her parental towards the other. She was his mother, and it was her duty to speak to him.

He came into the kitchen and sat down in the armchair, flinging his hat on to the edge of the table. He looked tired and depressed.

"Derek Smith," said his mother firmly, "where've you been?"

"Pompey," answered Derek sullenly. "I told you."

"And where was you the night before, when you didn't come in, and plenty of other times I'm not mentionin'?"

His resistance was breaking so he didn't answer.

"When you're livin' in this 'ouse," went on Mrs. Smith, "I've got a right to know where you are, and when you're comin' in to meals and when you're not. Your Dad don't like your ways and I don't neither."

"I'll be glad when this flamin' leave's over," said Derek miserably. "Things 'ave been bad enough without your goin' on at me, too."

The instinct to comfort and shield him was strong. Mrs. Smith made a shot in the dark.

"It's not that Miss Mackenzie, is it?" she asked.

It was on the tip of his tongue to tell his mother the whole story, but he knew he couldn't hope to make her understand. She had no sympathy for drinking, and she would be upset, and besides, it didn't do to bring Freda into it. She wouldn't comprehend that to have an affair with a girl like Freda wasn't wrong.

"No," he said, "I ain't seen 'er for a long time."

"I just wondered, that's all," said Mrs. Smith. "Tell your old Mum what's the matter, Derry?"

"It's nothin'," he said. "I'm just chokka. I told you I didn't want no naggin'." He stood up. "I'm goin' to paint the door." He announced this briefly, as embarrassed as she was by the sacrifice of the decision. "Where's Dad keep the brushes?"

She glanced at the clock. It was opening time. "Now?" she asked ungraciously.

Derek grinned in spite of himself.

"Now," he assented. "Can't afford dinner this morning." This cynicism of his mother's amused him and restored his good humour.

He found a blow-lamp, changed into his father's overalls, and began to strip the front door of its old brown paint. As his mother put the cake into the oven, she heard him whistling on the step.

V

It was Tuesday and so Freda was on duty in the girls' playground. She had forced herself not to think of Derek or the misery of yesterday, which was difficult for she was inclined to be both sentimental and to overanalyse situations. She had tried to convince herself it was a mistake and that Derek would telephone her. She would have been wiser to have gone out to a cinema when she had returned from Portsmouth, but she had sat at home, in case he called. He had not done so, nor had he rung this morning before she left for school. If he doesn't 'phone tonight, she thought, then I'll know it is the end.

She had applied herself to her class and lessons with determination.

"Miss?" said Joan Smith, who was waiting to take Freda's empty tea-cup back to the staff room, a task which was coveted, though Freda could never understand why. "It's my birthday tomorrow."

"Is it?" said Freda, smiling at her. "Then you'll be fifteen. School-days nearly over, Joan."

"Miss?" Joan paused, embarrassed, then took courage. "Miss, would you come to my party?"

Freda could feel herself blushing at the prospect.

"I don't think I can, Joan," she said, her voice restrained. "I'm going out tomorrow evening. But it's very kind of you to think of asking me."

"It's not the evenin', Miss," assured Joan, her face falling. "It's just for tea. You could go afterwards, Miss."

I can't go, thought Freda. How can I possibly go? If Derek hasn't contacted me by then, it would be throwing myself at him. It's out of the question.

"Miss, you are mean." Gladys Butler had been hovering on the fringe of the conversation, ready to enter into it. "She's leavin' at the end of the term, and she's been first for two weeks. You aren't 'alf mean, Miss Mackenzie. I don't know why some girls like bein' in your class."

"*Please*, Miss," urged Joan again. "It's my *birthday*."

" 'Er brother'll be there," added Gladys temptingly.

"All right, Joan. I'd love to come for a little while. Thank you."

"Miss, you're smashin'," asserted Gladys. " 'Ere," she called out, "Miss's goin' to Joan's birthday party."

"Will you come to mine when I 'ave one?" begged Doris Lacey ingratiatingly at Freda's side. She was besieged with invitations.

"I'll see," said Freda, smiling, and enjoying this temporary popularity. "I'll see when the time comes."

"You promised Joan," Gladys threatened her. "Don't go and say tomorrow you didn't, Miss. I 'eard yer."

It was nine o'clock or thereabouts and there was no sign of
Derek. Freda was tormenting herself. Was he with another girl,
or worse still, with those men? Was he having a gay and amusing
time, having forgotten all about her? Was he still in Portsmouth,
or was he back in London, perhaps only a few miles away, in the
West End? The desire to know was suddenly irresistible. I have to
find out, she said to herself. It's upsetting me too much. I can't go
on waiting for him to 'phone night after night. If it is finished, then
I must try and put him out of my mind.

She brushed her hair and put on her coat and went out into
Bannerton Gardens. Already along the benches the tramps were
settling down for the night. It always seemed incongruous, these
ragged homeless men and women sleeping in the respectable
streets of self-conscious Kensington. She was surprised the law
didn't move them on, but let them rest there with their newspaper
covers and paper-bags and sticks.

She took the train to Piccadilly and walked swiftly up Shaftesbury Avenue. Piccadilly at night frightened her. All the strange
unreal people who hid in the day roamed the streets. Night and
day each have a different congregation, she thought. Day people
were at home now, listening to the wireless or watching the television or working in their gardens. The night people were out, just
out and aimless.

From outside the Rob Roy the tinny piano sounded unmelo-
dious and harsh. The frosted windows revealed shadow heads,
moving back and forth, or still, in conversation.

Freda pushed open the door and went in. It was as crowded as
it had always been. It wasn't a Saturday-night pub, but an all-the-
week one. No one took any notice of her. Davy was leaning across
the bar talking to a well-known politician. Two soldiers, their
berets adorned by brightly-coloured hackles, stood near, smiling
across the scratched wood of the bar at an expensively dressed
woman with too much make-up. A slim girl in black, very tall with
gamin hair, was edging her way round the walls, looking at the
photographs and playbills, occasionally calling out to her escort
when one amused or surprised her. Over in the corner where
the bar curved round and hid the customers from the rest of the

room, just visible over the heads, was a sailor hat, shining, white, jaunty.

It was a chance in a thousand, but it might be Derek.

As Freda pushed her way through the crowd her heart thumped so she felt people must notice it. She wished she hadn't acted on her impulse to come. Suppose it was Derek? What was she going to say?

But the hat did not belong to Derek. It belonged to Johnnie.

"Johnnie!" cried Freda, hating him. "Where's Derek?"

He turned and saw her.

" 'Allo!" he said, taken by surprise. "What you doin ere?"

"I've come to look for Derek," she said simply. "Have you seen him?"

" 'Ave a drink?" suggested Johnnie. It was the panacea for all ills.

"I'm not here to drink," Freda said, her voice unnaturally high. "I'm looking for Derek." She made an effort to calm herself. "Have you seen him, Johnnie? I thought he might be here."

"No," Johnnie said, thinking Derek was well out of it. "I ain't seen 'im since yesterday. 'E came with us to Southsea, and then 'e lost 'imself." He suspected Derek had found himself a more absorbing pastime than Freda, but he didn't mention it. He didn't think Freda had anything to offer Derek, and he therefore assumed Derek was bored.

"Do you know where he might be?" Freda persisted. "Please think, Johnnie." If this got back to Derek, he would never forgive her.

"Well," he pushed his cap back and rubbed his brow. " 'E might be over in Sandy's Bar."

"Where's that?"

"Soho. Not far."

"Tell me how to get there?" She buttoned the neck of her coat again and put on the one glove she had taken off.

"I'll take you." Johnnie had nothing better to do, and it was a dead loss here tonight. He could have a look in Sandy's himself.

They did not speak as they hurried through the narrow streets. Little groups of prostitutes gathered at corners, and then split up again into ones and twos, all tastes catered for. It reminded Freda

of a particular day in her childhood when she went out to buy
a fairy doll for the Christmas tree. She had gone alone, and she
had had the money in her pocket. When she had entered the shop
the choice was so vast, red-headed girl dolls, golden-headed fairy
dolls, bald rubber baby dolls, fuzzy-haired black dolls, that she
had wandered up and down the show-cases for three-quarters of
an hour, deciding. She was limited by the money her father had
given her, and she had not bought a fairy doll at all, but a pigtailed
schoolgirl one.

She looked curiously at a man lingering on the pavement and
wondered if the sensation he was experiencing now was anything
akin to hers in the toy shop, and decided it must be. It was a thought
she would like to have voiced, and had it been Matthew at her side,
or Derek, she would have done so, but Johnnie had assumed an
expression of such sternness (perhaps because the temptations of
the street were rather hard to bear) that she held her tongue.

" 'Ere we are," he said brusquely. "It's down 'ere."

He indicated a doorway with stairs leading down to a basement.
Over the door was a blue neon sign that said 'Sandy's. Free House.'

"Want me to look for you?" he asked.

"No thank you." Freda wanted nothing more from Johnnie.

"I'll come with you then?"

"If you like." She had already begun to go down the stairs to the
bar. It was hot and stuffy, and the swing door at the foot was held
open by a man leaning against it.

As Freda entered, closely followed by Johnnie, she realized that
this pub was nothing like the Rob Roy. There were no aesthetes
and there were no women. The bar itself was in the centre of the
floor, an ellipse trapping two women in white overalls.

"What you goin' to 'ave for the lady?" one of them asked
Johnnie. "Horange?" She looked disapprovingly at him. "There's
a nice lounge room for ladies at the back," she said pointedly. "It's
all men in 'ere."

This was a part of London life Freda did not know existed, or if
she did, thought it was only in the slum areas round the docks, in
Cable Street and its environs. She turned to speak to Johnnie, but
he had become separated from her.

"Johnnie," she called out.

Two or three men, astonished at seeing her here, stood aside to let her pass with self-conscious politeness.

"Johnnie," she said, suddenly glad to have him with her, "he's not here, is he? I'm going. It's horrid."

"I'll give you a cup of coffee," he offered. She probably needed a cup of coffee, she seemed a bit edgy and she was a friend of Smudge's. Besides, he was a trifle curious about her.

"Thank you, Johnnie," she said gratefully. "I'd like one."

It was just on closing time, and the pubs were emptying into the streets. The milk-bars swallowed up the people as they came out of the saloons, and Freda found herself crushed in the crowd pushing with her into The Little Hen.

"Wait 'ere," Johnnie ordered her. "I'll get the coffee. Want anythin' to eat?"

"No thank you." She was elbowed to one side and stood back against the shiny yellow wall, looking at the reflection of the milk-bar in the smeared mirrors. Round the wall ran a plastic and chromium ledge littered with half-eaten food, piles of cups, cigarette butts awash in the cold slops. The whole bar was illuminated by the sickening garishness of yellow, pink and green strip lighting. Freda caught her own reflection. How out of place she seemed. What was she doing here? She was filled with disgust and longed for her flat, which she had sometimes considered bourgeois, and for her comfortable conventional home in Kent.

As she stood there an old woman in bundled rusty clothes came and asked her for a match.

"I'm sorry," said Freda. "I haven't one."

"You've got a kind face, dearie," said the woman tritely, and moved on.

Freda looked to see if Johnnie was still at the bar, and he was waiting to be served, engrossed in conversation with an airman.

"Nice evening?" said a young American in a powder-blue suit, with stains on the lapels. He stared unblinkingly as he said the words.

Freda turned her back and he walked away. It's like a grotesque cocktail party, she thought, a constant useless contact with people who talk, and go on to talk to someone else. Never alone for long, never together long enough.

" 'Ere we are," said Johnnie. "Drink up."

She sipped the coffee in the plastic cup. She felt she must talk to Johnnie who had been very sweet to her really, but she had nothing to say.

"You know," said Johnnie suddenly. "I shouldn't worry about old Smudge, if I was you. 'E's probably enjoyin' 'imself somewhere."

"Johnnie," she said, "I've never felt like this over anyone before."

He was taken off his guard. She'd no right to be soft over Smudge, a girl like her. He had a mental picture of Smudge at this moment with another party.

"You know sailors . . ." he began, embarrassed. It was small comfort.

"It's different this time," Freda said fiercely. "With me, Derek's quite different. You don't understand. Derek and I mean something to each other, and, Johnnie, it's places like this. I don't want him always to come to places like this, or like that bar, or like the Rob Roy. It was all right until we got to Portsmouth."

"Oh, I dunno," said Johnnie. What was wrong with places like this? It was an ordinary milk-bar, wasn't it? What did she expect? The Ritz?

"I wish we'd never gone there," said Freda. "He was all right till then."

"Oh well," said Johnnie uncomfortably. "I reckon 'e'll come back."

But Freda was finding it a relief to talk about Derek. Until now she had had no one with whom to discuss him.

"Johnnie?" she asked, probing. "Has Derek ever talked to you about me?"

He shook his head.

"No," he said. " 'E never said nothin' to me, but then I 'aven't seen 'im much."

Freda had been feeling wretched and miserable since yesterday, and now suddenly she felt she was going to cry. She finished her coffee and put the cup down on the ledge beside her. Johnnie seized the opportunity.

"Where do you live?" he asked her. "It's gettin' on. You don't want to miss the bus." If you ain't missed it already, he added to himself, pleased at the joke.

"Kensington. I can get a train. I think I'll go now, to be on the safe side."

"Yeah, you do that. And 'ave a good sleep. You'll feel better in the mornin'."

He couldn't wait to get her on the train. If she didn't go soon, it would be too late to get himself fixed up for tonight, and he'd have to go back to his own place, and he didn't want to do that.

"Mind if I don't come down the Underground with you?" he asked.

"No, of course I don't. Thank you, Johnnie. It's made me feel much better talking to you like this."

He took her to the station and left her at the top of the stairs. Smudge must be off his rocker, he concluded, walking back to the milk-bar, which was as good a place as any, getting caught up with a bint like her.

"Making for anywhere special, Jack?" said a voice at his side. Johnnie turned round, relieved. The evening hadn't been a complete waste after all.

VI

Joan Smith was in a state of extreme excitement. Having a birthday and a party gave her momentary prestige in the class. Her cards were passed from desk to desk, admired and envied and read aloud.

"The words ain't 'alf lovely," sighed Doreen rapturously. "'Ave you seen 'em, Miss?"

Joan gathered the cards from the corners of the room and placed them proudly on Freda's desk. The top one was from Derek, To My Sister, and had a picture of a girl playing tennis, a spaniel dog at her heels, and Happy Birthday Sis, written in printed gold longhand.

"She's 'ad some presents, too," called out Gladys.

"She's very lucky. What have you had, Joan?"

"Oh, all sorts of things, Miss. I'll show you when we gets 'ome, shall I?" She became rather shy, thinking of Miss at home.

"I'd like to see them. There's the bell now. Line up. No talking."

Prayers were held in the hall, and the hall was also used for gym. During the hymn Freda found herself staring up at the looped ropes and thinking of Derek. It was two days since she had seen him. Did he know, she wondered, that she would be at Joan's tea party? Did he mind? How would he behave?

"I'm waiting for Gladys Butler to stop talking before I begin the Lord's Prayer," said Miss Carstairs from the rostrum.

Freda came sharply back to earth, and fixed the grinning Gladys with a cold stare.

"Heads bowed, eyes closed," instructed Miss Carstairs. This did not apply to the staff. The staff had to keep an acute vigilance.

"Our Father," intoned Miss Carstairs.

"Our Father," mumbled the school.

Prayers over, the lessons began. Freda was in favour today, because she had promised to go to the Smiths' for tea. Her class was quiet and well behaved. How sweet they can be when they want, she thought. She felt quite proud when Miss Carstairs came in suddenly, and saw the rows of industrious home-permed heads over the desks.

Joan went home at dinner time and returned to school in her birthday frock, a low-cut black taffeta which lay flatly on her chest. When lessons ended she clipped on a pair of diamante ear-rings and applied a little lipstick. Her nylons had butterfly clocks.

"Miss, my brother give me these," she said, drawing up her skirt to show Freda. " 'E bring 'em 'ome dinner time."

The gulf between Derek's taste in these matters and his natural enjoyment of good things, be it music or her own clothes, seemed incredible to Freda.

"You ready, Miss?" asked Joan.

The other party-goers, festively clad like their hostess, hovered round Freda self-consciously.

"Yes. Give me a few minutes to tidy up and I'll be with you."

She hurried into the staff room, powdered her nose and combed her hair. The nearness of her meeting with Derek made her excited and apprehensive, in spite of her reasoning. She joined the seven girls again, and they clattered down to the playground ahead of her, breaking the embarrassed silence with occasional giggles. They tottered along Jubilee Road in their high heels, nudging each other and making silly remarks. At number twenty-three Joan pushed open the gate and they trooped to the front door.

"Mind the paint," warned Joan. It shone a bright wet green.

They gathered up their skirts and passed into the narrow brown-papered hallway one at a time, ushering Freda first.

Mrs. Smith came from the kitchen. She was wearing a beige dress with an elaborately frilled collar fastened by a large brooch of multi-coloured stones. Her hair was pinned in tight curls. She was obviously dressed for the occasion.

"Mum," said Joan. "This is our teacher."

Mrs. Smith pursed her lips slightly.

"Pleased to meet you, Miss Mackenzie," she said without warmth. "Joan's spoke ever so 'ighly of you."

So that's her, is it? she thought. Scheming creature. Whatever Derry said she didn't believe he wasn't staying out nights because of her. Why couldn't she stick to boys of her own class?

Freda felt conscious of the close scrutiny. Just what I thought, she said to herself, clean and respectable, yet as different from Derek in her way as I am. It puzzled her that a boy from this environment could have his charms and possibilities. It wasn't as if he had gone to a Grammar School.

"'Allo, Miss Mackenzie." It was his voice, deliberately casual. He was coming down the stairs.

She turned and saw him. He was out of uniform. He was wearing his best suit of fawn gaberdine with a maroon and blue patterned American tie and chocolate-brown suede shoes with a criss-cross pattern on the toes. Freda was astonished how ordinary he looked.

"Hallo, Derek," she said, her own voice casual too.

"Come in, everybody," said Joan. "Tea's all ready."

"'Allo, Derek Smith," bridled Gladys. "In yer birthday suit?"

"You are awfu'," tittered Doris.

"I got a better one than this upstairs," Derek rallied happily.

"Now then, now then," said Mrs. Smith.

They crowded into the front room where the table was spread with birthday fare. Like most of the front rooms in Jubilee Road it was occupied only on rare occasions like Christmas and birthday parties, and briefly on Thursday afternoons when the Insurance man called. It was furnished with a three-piece suite covered in brown rexine, and orange satin cushions had been placed carefully one on each chair, and on the corners of the sofa. On the far wall hung a picture of a three-masted barque in full sail, while over the mantelpiece a heavy Victorian frame encircled a self-conscious wedding group, dressed in comically outdated clothes.

In the centre of the table was a pink-iced birthday-cake with JOAN worked out in pieces of fruit gum. There were orange jellies with orange segments on them, sausage rolls and jam sandwiches, and a dish of fondants and all Joan's cards standing by her plate.

"You sit 'ere, Miss Mackenzie," said Mrs. Smith, "and you come down next to your sister, Derry." She wasn't going to put them together, making a set at her Derry like that.

"I want to sit next to Miss," claimed Doreen.

They all sat down.

Mrs. Smith poured tea for everyone from a large brown pot into an assortment of cups. There was a rustle of paper serviettes.

"You tuck yours up, Joanie," said Mrs. Smith, "if you think you're goin' dancin' in that dress."

"Oh, Mum," said Joan.

"What'll you 'ave, Miss Mackenzie?" asked Derek. Their eyes met over the plate of sandwiches he held out to her.

Conversation, which had been stilted, was all at once wild and unleashed. Freda felt she ought to control the girls. The subject somehow got on to babies, and Gladys Butler became carried away with her own humour. But she was out of school now. Freda smiled, and attempted to steer the conversation. She mustn't dampen the party. It was very nice of Joan to ask her, and she couldn't treat the girls as if they were in the classroom.

"They become high-spirited on occasions like this," she excused them to Mrs. Smith.

"And quite right too," rebuked Mrs. Smith. "If you don't enjoy yourself when you're young when do you, I say?"

The time had arrived for Joan to cut the cake. Derek lit the candles for her, and the sight of his masculine hand steadily holding the match made Freda suddenly realize that whether in uniform or not, he still retained an immense physical attraction for her. She had resigned herself to the fact that their affair was over, but even in that dreadful suit he disturbed her unaccountably.

On any other occasion she would have enjoyed Joan's birthday, and have found it fun and friendly. Now she was aware of a hostile undercurrent from Mrs. Smith, and she was uncomfortable for Derek, the way he joined the girls in silly suggestive jokes.

As soon as tea was over, she stood up and excused herself.

"It was a lovely party, Joan. Thank you for letting me come, Mrs. Smith. See you all tomorrow. Goodbye, Derek."

She put on her coat and Joan saw her to the door.

"It was lovely 'avin' you, Miss. We're goin' to play a few games, and then I'm goin' dancin' tonight."

Freda said goodbye again and walked back up Jubilee Road to the bus-stop outside the school. To think it was here that she had first really spoken to Derek. The inconclusiveness of their meeting this afternoon filled her with frustration and wretchedness.

"Freda!"

She turned round. He had come after her.

"Derek!"

He ran up to her, and took her hands.

"Don't go yet," he said. " 'Ang on five minutes, and I'll be with you."

"What about the party?"

"That can go on without me. We'll go to the pictures, eh? There's a good film on at the local."

"I'd love to."

"Freda?"

"Yes?"

"I looked all over for you in Pompey. I didn't mean to lose you. I looked in every flippin' pub there was."

"Did you, Derek?"

"I 'aven't rung you. It's because I've been skint."

"Oh, Derek." She looked at him tenderly. "What difference does that make?"

"It makes a difference to me," he said doggedly. "I won't be a sec." He let go of her hands and ran back up the street.

As he ran he told himself he was crazy. What was the point of starting it up again? She wouldn't say yes last time, and she wasn't likely to say it again now. But she'd looked so smashing sitting up at the table next to all those girls, and when she spoke to him she had seemed so far away he couldn't bear it. He thought of her making love to him that night and his desire mounted.

It was no use getting away from it. He wanted her, and he didn't want anybody else, that was straight. She was so different from everyone. He had to take her out tonight, if it was the last time he ever did.

"Mum," he said, "lend us another ten bob. I'm goin' to the flicks."

He went upstairs two at a time, and combed his hair carefully in front of the mirror. Then on an impulse he changed back into his uniform. She liked his uniform. With all its drawbacks square rig had its uses. It was murder to put on and take off, but given the right circumstances it was as good as a love potion.

Let's hope it works tonight, he said to himself, tying his lanyard.

In the darkness of the cinema Derek put his arm along Freda's shoulders, and turned her face to his with a gentle pressure of his hand on her neck. For a brief moment Freda resisted, but it was only for a moment. Then she turned to him and as they kissed she realized that her feeling hadn't changed, and that from now on she would make no effort to keep away from him.

"Freda," he said suddenly. "I got three days left."

"I know," she said.

"Come on," he said urgently. "Let's go. We don't want to see this."

Holding her hand he led her impatiently along the row of people without waiting for them to stand and let them pass. They hurried up the aisle into the foyer where angled coloured photographs of film stars hung on the green and buff walls.

"Where?" he asked. "Your flat?"

She nodded, their eyes met and they both smiled.

"Okay? You ready? Don't want to comb your 'air or anythin'?"

"No."

"'Allo, Miss." They turned round. It was Doris Lacey. "'Allo, Derek Smith," she smirked. "Enjoy the pitcher? Eh?" She burst into a shrill laugh, and clutching her small brother's hand disappeared through the swing doors with a triumphant flounce.

"Oh God," said Freda, "that's done it. They'll all know in the morning."

They walked along Whitechapel Road where one or two of the market stalls were only now just packing up for the night. A little way ahead on the other side of the street the lights were beginning to appear in the windows of London Hospital. It was the hospital where Matthew worked, and Freda could not help looking to see if his car was parked in one of the side roads. Derek put his arm through hers, and held her close as if he could not be near enough to her. They scarcely spoke as they walked, and on the train they held hands tightly, and smiled once or twice, but that was all. As they hurried along Bannerton Gardens their silence seemed somehow to intensify their closeness to each other. Freda's hand was trembling slightly as she put the key into the lock. It seemed a long time before she had turned the key, opened the door, entered. Then she closed it behind them and ran the bolt across.

They were in one another's arms at last, kissing, caressing, breathless. They stood embracing for some minutes still in their outdoor clothes. Then Derek suddenly released her and taking off his hat walked to the open window. A light wind disturbed his hair and a lamp across the gardens shone palely on his temple. He leaned against the sill and stared out on to the dark tops of the trees.

"You don't know what you done to me," he said. "I thought we'd never be like this again."

"Draw the curtains," said Freda after a second, "and I'll put on the light."

He closed the window and drew the curtains across, turning to watch her. She switched on the lamp beside the bed, took off her

coat, and knelt down to light the gas fire which popped and sput-
tered, its flames encompassing all the colours of the spectrum.

"Give me your raincoat," she said. He gave it to her and she
hung both their coats on the back of the door, one on top of the
other. "Something to eat?"

He shook his head, then moved across the room and took her
hand.

"Let's go to bed," he said.

Freda woke up because Derek was kissing her. Still half asleep
she put her arms round him and lay still.

"What's the time?" she asked.

"Nearly seven."

"So you stayed the night after all. You won."

"How about breakfast?" he asked.

Freda stretched. "Derek, hasn't it been fun? Hasn't it been
wonderful?"

"Yes it 'as. And I've got three days, countin' today."

"I've got an idea." Freda tied the cord of her dressing-gown and
went into the kitchenette.

"Yes?" He sat up, hugging his knees.

"I've got to go home this weekend. Will you come down on
Saturday for the day, and I'll come back to London with you. I
won't stay the whole weekend, then we can have Saturday night
together."

"What? Me come 'ome with you?" He was aghast. "What would
your Mum say?"

"She won't mind. She'll understand, I'll talk to her first. I won't
say we're lovers, of course." She liked saying 'lovers'. The word
was romantic, improper, suggesting soft lights, naked bodies and
impromptu meals on the edge of the bed. "I'll just say you're Joan's
brother. Please, Derek, will you?"

"If you're sure it'll be okay?"

"Yes I am."

"All right then. If you really mean it."

They ate their breakfast and Freda got ready for school.

"I'll 'ave a bath," said Derek. "I'll be careful not to let the old girl see me when I go." He kissed her affectionately. "Be good. I'll pick you up at school, four-thirty."

After she had gone he took his bath. His blue towel still hung on the rail. He felt extremely pleased with life. It had turned out to be a good leave after all, though it hadn't looked like it a day or two ago. Whoever would have thought he'd fall in love with a schoolteacher. It just showed, you never knew what was round the corner for you. Life was full of surprises.

VII

"Do try to be intelligent," said Freda to Gladys Butler. "Don't you ever listen to what I tell you?"

"Miss's cross this mornin', ain't she?" demanded Doreen of the class at large. "I reckon she didn't 'ave enough sleep larse night." She sniggered.

There was no doubt about it. They all knew. Doris had arrived early, almost the first person in the building, and as the class appeared, one by one, so they had formed an excited group in the cloakroom, probing Doris for the last scraps of information.

"I've finished with Miss, straight," Doris muttered now, glowering at Freda. "She needn't think I'm goin' to ask 'er to *my* birfday party, 'cos I ain't."

"Never known you 'ave a birfday party," retorted Gladys, who liked to be fair. "Your Mum's too flippin' mean. Couple of left-over kippers all you'd get in that 'ouse." The class cackled.

"Will you all be quiet," snapped Freda, her voice raised. "Or I shall be really angry."

" 'Ark at 'er, Glad!"

Laughter broke out, then abruptly ceased. The girls were suddenly subdued.

"That's better." Miss Carstairs had come into the room unobserved to Freda. "Miss Mackenzie, could you spare me a moment?"

"Certainly." Freda stood up. "Gladys, come out to the front, and if anyone talks send them outside."

Gladys giggled with self-conscious pleasure at being singled out for responsibility, and made her way to Freda's desk. She stood waiting for the two teachers to depart, in order that she might do her imitation of Miss Parrot.

No sooner were Miss Carstairs and Freda in the corridor, than a roar of appreciation reached their ears.

"I'll go on to the study," said Miss Carstairs. "Come along when you're ready."

Freda spoke severely to her class, threatened them with no break, and then withdrew again, still wondering why Miss Carstairs wanted her.

She knocked at the study door.

"Come in," said the headmistress.

In front of the desk, in almost the same spot where Derek had stood that first afternoon, was a nondescript middle-aged woman. Her face was round and her small eyes shone like burnt currants. Her mouth was small too, and insofar as the thin compressed lips could be said to register an expression, it seemed to Freda most nearly to resemble a righteous smirk. Several inches of flowered apron showed beneath her coat.

"Ah, Miss Mackenzie," Miss Carstairs said, "this is Mrs. Lacey."

"How do you do?" said Freda formally.

Mrs. Lacey pointedly ignored the introduction.

"I'm afraid this is rather an unhappy matter, Miss Mackenzie," Miss Carstairs said. "Mrs. Lacey has made some accusations concerning you and naturally I wanted you to be here."

"What sort of accusations?" asked Freda, looking straight at Mrs. Lacey. Freda's composure made Mrs. Lacey less sure of her ground, so when she spoke she didn't look at Freda, but talked directly to Miss Carstairs.

"It's about 'er carryin' on with Derek Smith, and I'm sure I don't mind sayin' it to 'er face neither. She's not fit to be teachin' young girls. 'E was my Maureen's boy and she's been runnin' after 'im since 'e been 'ome. It's my opinion she done it deliberate to spite Maureen. Doris see 'em together in the pitchers larse night, and I said to Mr. Lacey, 'I'm goin' straight up to see Miss Carstairs in the mornin' and 'ave it out with 'er'."

"Is that all?" said Freda. "There's quite a simple explanation. I went to Joan Smith's birthday tea, as you probably know, and afterwards I went on to the cinema where I met Derek Smith. But I really don't see why I should justify the way in which I spent my evening."

Miss Carstairs turned to Mrs. Lacey.

"You see, your fears are groundless. I have the utmost faith in Miss Mackenzie both as a teacher and as a moral influence."

Mrs. Lacey appeared disappointed that her revelations had not had a more explosive effect. She took a deep breath and clasped her hands in front of her.

"I'm not leavin' this room until I 'ave an understandin' that she don't see Derek Smith no more."

Miss Carstairs cut her short.

"Really, Mrs. Lacey," she said. "I cannot interfere in any way with the personal affairs of my staff. If Miss Mackenzie wishes to speak to Derek Smith, that is her own business, and from the school's point of view her behaviour is perfectly acceptable." She turned her attention to Freda. "I'm sorry to have disturbed your lesson, Miss Mackenzie, I'm sure you want to get back to it. I shall be free during break if you'd like to see me."

"Thank you, Miss Carstairs," said Freda, opening the door. She didn't doubt that Miss Carstairs was more than capable of dealing with Mrs. Lacey's refusal to leave without an 'understanding'.

Not a sound came from behind the closed door of her classroom. But when she entered the first thing she saw, in the large uneven handwriting of someone unused to a blackboard, were the words 'All the nice girls love a sailor' and underneath a drawing evidently meant to be her head and Derek's some inches apart, the mouths protruding into a pouting kiss.

"It wasn't me, Miss," said Gladys Butler smugly, interpreting Freda's glance. "And I didn't see 'oo did it, neither." She appealed to the class. "Did you, girls?"

"No," they chorused. "It wasn't none of us, Miss."

"Does 'e 'old you nice?" asked Doreen, so impertinently that Freda would have liked to hit her. "I bet 'e does. 'Im a sailor, Miss."

"You've asked for it," said Freda. "None of you is going out during playtime, this morning or afternoon. And if I have any more of this, I shall keep you in after school as well."

But I wouldn't really, she told herself, because I'd miss being with Derek. Punishment after school can wait until next week.

As soon as she had settled the girls with extra work, Freda went back to Miss Carstairs's study, feeling she must make an effort to clear the matter up.

"I'm sorry about this morning," she said to Miss Carstairs, closing the door behind her.

"Mrs. Lacey was quite difficult, wasn't she?" observed Miss Carstairs, stirring her tea. "But I feel I must warn you, Miss Mackenzie, that in a school of this kind it really is wiser not to make friends of the girls or their families. It is bound to arouse petty jealousies."

"I realize that now," said Freda. "I shall take good care in future."

"Have you seen much of Derek Smith?" Miss Carstairs asked suddenly, just as Freda was about to go.

"Only once or twice," said Freda. "He's very intelligent, you know. I took him to a concert. Not," she added, smiling, "to spite Maureen Lacey."

Miss Carstairs smiled back. "You won't get Mrs. Lacey to believe that. But forewarned is forearmed, Miss Mackenzie. It isn't worth the ensuing trouble, I can assure you."

"I won't make the mistake again," Freda promised. And went back to her class.

During lunch hour, her sandwiches eaten and the story of Mrs. Lacey now staff room knowledge, and a source of great amusement, Freda hurried along Jubilee Road to the Smiths' house to see Derek. The last thing in the world she wanted now was to find him outside the school at half-past four.

She knocked at the green front door, and heard Joan's voice calling from upstairs.

"Someone at the door, Mum."

After a few moments it was opened by Mrs. Smith.

"I wondered if I dropped my watch here yesterday," said Freda.

"I thought I had it when I left, but I've asked at the Underground and it hasn't been handed in."

"Come in while I 'as a look," said Mrs. Smith. "I've swept up in there, but you can never tell."

They went together into the front room. The leaves of the light oak table had been pushed in, and a gold satin runner ran diagonally across it, weighted in the middle by a blue glass bowl which yesterday had been full of trifle, but now held everlasting flowers.

Mrs. Smith shook the cushions, and pushed her hand down the sides of the chairs and sofa.

"No," she said, "it don't seem to be 'ere. If I comes across it, I'll send Joanie up the school with it."

"Thank you," said Freda, wondering what oblique message she could leave for Derek, so that he would know not to meet her as they had arranged.

"I suppose Derek won't be back yet awhile, will he, Mrs. Smith? I would have liked to wish him good luck. He's back to the navy in a day or so, isn't he?"

"That's right," assented Mrs. Smith. She knows all right when he's going back, she said inwardly. Pretending she doesn't. Who does she think I am, not knowing what my son's up to? I'd like to give her a piece of my mind.

"He was going to come up to the school this afternoon to say goodbye to me," said Freda. "I've got a book on music I want to lend him. But I shan't be at school after lunch, so would you mind telling him that if he still wants it, he can collect it from my rooms at about half-past five this evening? I'll give you the address."

She wrote it down on a piece of exercise-book paper, torn from one of the composition books she had under her arm.

"I should've thought 'e knew your address," commented Mrs. Smith, "seein' as 'ow 'e 'ad supper with you one night."

"I don't for one minute expect he remembers it," said Freda, taken by surprise. "I met him at the Underground station and took him back. I'm certain he wouldn't have noticed the name of the road, let alone the number of the house."

"Well, I'll tell 'im your message," said Mrs. Smith. "And I'll 'ave another look for your watch."

"Thank you," Freda said, sorry that she hadn't been able to break down Mrs. Smith's antagonism. She would have liked to have talked to her about Derek. She glanced at the carved wooden clock on the mantelpiece. "Heavens, how late it is. I must get back."

Thought you wasn't going to be at school this afternoon, said Mrs. Smith to herself. But she said nothing to Freda, or to Derek when he came in five minutes later, except to give him the message, which he received non-committally as he ate his dinner.

"You know," she said to her husband, who had come back early, and thinking Derek was asleep in the chair, "I wish Derry'd tell me more about 'is girls. 'E's gone and dropped that nice Maureen, and now 'e's carryin' on with Joanie's teacher. I can't say I like it."

"Joan's teacher, is it?" said Mr. Smith tolerantly. "Well I never! It takes a sailor to get around, don't it?"

"Not 'alf it don't," thought Derek.

VIII

After Freda had left for school on Friday morning, taking her weekend case with her, Derek tidied up the flat, and enjoyed his role of domesticity. He made the bed, washed up the breakfast crockery, emptied the ashtray, dusted the furniture. He sang as he worked. He had had fun the last few days. He couldn't remember a more exciting leave. He never thought he would enjoy the intimacy of doing out her flat, knowing that the plates went here, the knives there. It was like being married, only he wasn't tied down. He realized with a stab of sadness and jealousy that if Freda had been his class, if it had been in any way remotely possible, he would have asked her to marry him. He knew that from now on he would want more from a girl than the Maureens of the world could give him. He needed someone like Freda, who was educated as well as a good lay. It gave him a feeling of pride when she talked to him in her lah-di-dah accent, and, as if there was no difference at all between them, asked him his advice as if he was the one who really knew best.

"Miss Mackenzie? Hallo, Miss Mackenzie, are you there?"

Derek froze in a ridiculous suspended pose, as if he had been caught by a camera shot, the duster in his hand held up to a picture, one foot slightly off the ground.

"Is that you, Miss Mackenzie?"

She'd heard him then. She hadn't just come upstairs on the off chance of finding Freda at home. He must have been mad to sing, bawling his head off like that. He realized now how strong his voice had been.

Mrs. Gibson-Brown knocked loudly and repeatedly on the door.

What shall I do? thought Derek. Remain silent and she'd probably call the police. Answer the door, and Freda would probably be kicked out of the house for having a man there. He brought the hand with the duster slowly down to his side. He moved across the room silently and stood by the door, still not knowing what to do. On the other side Mrs. Gibson-Brown started to knock again.

"Miss Mackenzie? Miss Mackenzie?"

Derek stretched out his fingers and curled them round the handle, and then, on an impulse, pulled the door sharply open. He and Mrs. Gibson-Brown faced each other hostilely across the threshold.

"Oh," Mrs. Gibson-Brown took a small step backwards. "I thought as much!"

"Did you want Miss Mackenzie?" asked Derek. "She ain't in."

"Who are you?" demanded Mrs. Gibson-Brown, then, answering herself, "You're the sailor I saw her with the other day. What are you doing here?"

"I'm an old boy out of Miss Mackenzie's class," invented Derek hopelessly. "She's 'ad to go off 'ome. I've come in to clean up 'er room for 'er."

Swallow that one, he thought, and you're a bigger mug than I took you for.

Mrs. Gibson-Brown stared at him searchingly. She could scarcely bear to bring out the words.

"Did I hear you up here last night, young man?"

"No, you didn't," said Derek. "What do you think Miss Mackenzie is? I come in ten minutes ago. I met 'er at the station like we arranged, and she give me the key to get in by."

You dirty-minded old so-and-so, he thought, wouldn't you just love me to say yes?

"I see." Mrs. Gibson-Brown turned to go downstairs. "You can tell Miss Mackenzie I don't approve of this at all. I shall see her on Monday evening."

"Don't approve of what?" called Derek after her. "Of 'er wantin' to keep the flat what she rents from you clean?"

He slammed the front door and leaned against it. Christ, what a thing to do! He shouldn't have answered the door. What would Freda say when he told her tomorrow? Perhaps I won't tell her till the last minute before I go, he thought. It'll only upset her and it's our last day together, I don't want to go and spoil it for her. I've spoilt enough as it is.

He went home at midday and packed his things.

"I'm goin' off early tomorrow," he said to his mother. He felt he had let her down this leave, and asked her whether the paint on the front door had dried properly, to remind her that he hadn't deserted her altogether.

"Yes, it's dried lovely," she said. "I thought you wasn't due back till Sunday late?"

"I'm not," said Derek guiltily. "I been asked to the country to a friend's 'ouse tomorrow, and I won't be back till Sunday. I'll collect my gear round about seven, that okay?"

He had intended to find Johnnie and have one last night out in town, but he changed his mind. He'd take Mum out to the flicks, Joanie too, if she was home, and then he'd have a couple of pints with the old man.

"But I'll be 'ere all day today," he added. "We can talk about Sunday later, eh, Mum? Leave's not up yet."

He put on a kettle of water so that he could have a shave before dinner, and went upstairs to change into civilian clothes.

IX

Freda made a 'phone call from Victoria Station to her parents' home in Kent. She generally did this on her way there, so that somebody would meet her by car the other end. She reversed the charges since she had no small change, and the male operator, recognizing a young voice, said "Poor old Dad."

It was in fact her father who answered the telephone and accepted the call. Yes, he'd be at the station to meet her. It was lucky she rang then or she would have missed him. He was just going up to the farm to collect a chicken for tomorrow's lunch.

Settled on the train, Freda took out her book, Turgenev's *On the Eve*, and attempted to read. Stories of ill-destined love had always moved her, and now more than ever. Why did people embark upon affairs that could only end unhappily? What demon force compelled them to go on when it was still possible to retract? What idiocy had possessed *her* to become Derek's mistress? She turned down the corner of the page and put the book away, having read only a paragraph.

She looked out of the window, but the scenery didn't register. The grey-green blur of fields put her into a kind of trance in which everything was visually hazy and her thoughts were almost dreamlike. She still experienced a warm contented afterglow that stemmed from physical love and affection. She imagined her inner warmth must also be apparent in her eyes. She had always found it a little embarrassing to observe the obvious happiness that some-times emanated from physically contented women, as though they were revealing a secret. See if you can keep it to yourself, she thought, you try to hide it! Even the truth that Derek would be gone the day after tomorrow had no proper reality, because tomorrow came in between.

Her thoughts went from past to future and back again, all centralizing round Derek. She built up scenes of introducing him to her family, to the moments afterwards when they were alone, quite possibly in the garden, then back to an embrace that had occurred a few days before, then on again to tomorrow night when they would be together in her flat.

The train drew up at the signals outside the station, and the noise as the train braked brought her sharply back to earth. She pulled her case down from the rack, found her ticket, and turned the door-handle, holding on to it so that the door would not

swing open until they were at the platform. Someone in the next
compartment started an impatient drumming with his feet. Every
sound carried clearly. Then the train jerked, and moved on into the
station. Freda climbed down, seeing the creeper round the name-
board, the three circular flower beds packed with white alyssum,
forget-me-nots and bright red wallflowers in that order in inward
progression, quite freshly, as Derek would see them tomorrow.

"Good evening, Bill," she said to the ticket collector, enjoying
being recognized and recognizing, and looking forward to sharing
all the familiar things with Derek.

In the station yard her father was sitting in their four-year-old
black Wolseley, his slightly Punch-like head poking out of the
window. He saw her and pressed the hooter.

"Hallo." Freda hurried her step and climbed in beside him,
heaving her case over both their shoulders on to the scratched
green upholstery of the back seat.

"Good week?" inquired her father, leaning across and slamming
the door. He was a retired stockbroker who had never known
dazzling success, but who took life without undue worry. His
fondness for Freda was never demonstrated, but she was always
aware of a strong bond between them.

"Not bad," she said. The understatement made her want to
giggle. It had swung from extremes of utter misery to peaks of
startling happiness.

"Did you enjoy the party?" her father asked, as they turned
from the main road into a narrow lane, where the low branches
brushed across the roof of the car.

"What party?" said Freda.

"I thought Margot said you went to a party."

"Oh yes, yes, I did. It seems ages ago. I'd forgotten I hadn't seen
you since. I enjoyed it."

Mr. Mackenzie switched on the radio for the sports news, and
drove on in silence, until they reached the house. He shut off the
engine and sat listening to the racing results a few moments longer,
before he turned the knob briskly and jumped out of the car.

Their house, a small Georgian one, faced what had once been
the village green, but during the war it had been ploughed up

and was still under cultivation, and now it was silvery green with young wheat. When Freda had been a child the road had been a rough stone track, generally full of potholes and puddles, and there had only been a few cottages besides their own house. But over the years the road had been asphalted and widened, small semi-detached houses had been built all along one side, and there was a bus-stop and shelter on the pavement outside the pub. The front and back windows of the Mackenzies' house still looked across fields and woods, but the side ones revealed a long suburban road.

Inside the house the rooms were high-ceilinged and regularly shaped, the furniture unelaborate and comfortable. There was nothing that could be labelled 'bad-taste', but there was no central idea behind the decoration. In the hall stood a round Regency table, but there was also a 1920 ottoman, with two cushions on it embroidered by Freda in her handwork class when she was thirteen. When the old curtains wore out, they were replaced by new ones of a similar colour and design.

Hearing the car Mrs. Mackenzie had come to the front door to greet them.

"Hallo, darling," she called, and came towards Freda to take her case from her. They kissed each other lightly.

"How nice the flowers look," said Freda, going into the house.

Mrs. Mackenzie was an intelligent, pretty woman who was growing fat. Well read, slightly arrogant and at times showing great insight into character and situation, she appeared immediately attractive. Hers was a very individual personality, whereas once away from their own particular friends, the personalities of both her husband and Freda would fade into the background. Her untidiness, her lack of interest in clothes, were in her endearing traits, not irritating ones.

"Would you like a bath before dinner?" she asked, putting down Freda's case just inside the door. "It won't be ready for half an hour."

"Yes, I would," said Freda. "I feel a bit tired." She went up to her room which still bore traces of her nursery days, for the frieze had not been properly painted out and faint black rabbits could be seen marching under the paint. She went along to the bathroom and turned on the hot tap, spread the tufted green bathmat and put her towel over the heated rail. The steam rose and settled over the mirrors and clung in little wet drops to the walls. She could smell the dinner cooking downstairs. Better than eggs and bacon on her own stove. It was lovely to be home and have life run for her, sheets changed, bed turned down, meals prepared. Perhaps this was the sort of life she liked best after all.

"Oh, by the way," said Freda—they had reached the sweet course—"I hope it's all right? I've asked someone down for the day tomorrow."

"Yes, that's all right," said Mrs. Mackenzie. "Who is it, Matthew?" She had always made a point of encouraging Freda to bring her friends home, for she felt that this would prevent the secret liaisons to which she had resorted when she was young.

"Don't mind," Freda warned her. "It's a boy from Jubilee Road."

"Oh, darling," said her mother. "Did you *have* to ask him?"

"Yes, you'll like him though. He's a brother of one of my girls, in the navy now. His name's Derek Smith."

"Some more fruit, dear? What time does he get here?"

"I'm meeting him off the eleven-thirty," said Freda. "No, no more, thank you. That was lovely. He won't stay late, Mummy. I've got to go back to town myself so it will be a good excuse to get him away too."

"What's he like?" asked Mrs. Mackenzie, curious that Freda should have invited him, yet bored by the thought of having to entertain someone who would perhaps not fit in easily.

"He's very intelligent," answered Freda, trying hard not to sound too enthusiastic, "and rather nice-looking. But of course he has never had a chance to develop."

"I think I shall go out for tea," said Mr. Mackenzie pointedly.

"Oh, Daddy, you are a snob," said Freda. "He's such a nice boy."

"You're a snob too," said her mother. "When you were at the university you wouldn't speak to anyone who hadn't read Kafka. Let's have coffee on the terrace. It's a lovely evening."

Freda took the car down to the station to meet Derek. Coming out into the small white-palinged yard and seeing her parked there, gave Derek his first intimation that the day wasn't going to be easy.

"I didn't know you drove a car," he said awkwardly, climbing in beside her. But at the same time he couldn't help thinking if he had her money he'd get something a bit smarter than this old bus.

"Yes," Freda smiled. "I only passed my test last holidays. It will be ages before I have a car of my own, though."

"This your Dad's then?"

She nodded, pressing the starter. "I'm always a bit jerky when I start off. Hang on tight." She let in the clutch and they lurched forward, circled the two battered station taxi-cabs and turned into the main road.

"Blimey," said Derek, "if we get there we shall be lucky."

"What did your Mum say," he asked after a moment, "when you told 'er I was comin' down?"

"Oh, Derek, you are funny. She didn't say anything. She likes me to invite my friends."

"Yeah, but I'm different, aren't I?" he pursued doggedly. "I'm not the same class as you." He didn't look at her as he spoke.

"Derek *darling*, she accepts my friends. Don't start being difficult, for heaven's sake."

As soon as they had turned into a quieter lane she stopped the car and put her hand in his.

"Derek, did you miss me yesterday?"

"Course I did." He was unrelaxed.

"Kiss me. I missed *you* terribly."

"I'll kiss you now," he said, "but I'm not goin' to kiss you at your 'ome." He had sudden pictures of Freda snatching every moment they were alone to embrace him, or even touching his hand surreptitiously when her parents were near. "I don't want anyone thinkin' anythin'."

"All right." She was amused at his determination, and certain she would change his resolution before long. "You are being firm today."

He took her into his arms, and both of them were suddenly overwhelmed at the pleasure of being together again. For Freda the familiar contact of his mouth, the feel and smell of his uniform, gave a sensation of excitement which left her breathless and trembling. After a minute or two she made an effort and pulled away from him.

"We mustn't be too long," she said, "or Daddy will think I've run the car into a ditch. You know," she said, as she started the car again, and as usual trying to analyse her emotions, "however exciting the early stages of an affair are, really *knowing* each other is best of all, isn't it?"

As they drove along the lane she pointed out landmarks to him.

"See that tree? I was stuck up it for two hours when I was eight. They had to fetch me down with a ladder.

"That's the field I generally go mushrooming in.

"This was where I turned off when I used to cycle to school."

These things were of no importance to Derek. He was interested in Freda now, not in a remote past, but she did not sense this and talked on happily, identifying the localities of her childhood. She wanted to know everything about *him* and was sure he must feel the same about the things that concerned her. She had always found it impossible to accept that her emotions were unshared. If she loved, she assumed love in return. If she felt unfriendly, she couldn't believe it was not being reciprocated.

"We're nearly there now," she said to prepare him. "And, Derek, my parents aren't a bit awe-inspiring."

"I can't 'elp feelin' a bit scared meetin' 'em," he said. "I feel I oughtn't to be 'ere."

"I tell you what," suggested Freda, "I'll show you round the garden first, and you can meet them later, when you're more at home. How's that?"

"Fine," he said.

They turned into the drive and pulled up, the gravel spinning out from under the wheels.

"This your 'ouse?" He looked at the square white façade with the black door and window frames, his disappointment scarcely concealed. "I thought it would be bigger."

It was curious, his disappointment. He supposed he should have been relieved to find she didn't live in a mansion, and her

Dad didn't have a flashy car, but it was a bit of a let-down, this flat, ordinary-looking house. He hadn't made a conscious effort to visualize her home, but an impression had formed in his mind that it would be rambling, with beams and red brick, and some sort of flowers growing over it. He'd rather have one of the new flats at Jubilee Road Corner where Maureen Lacey lived.

Freda took him round the side of the house into the garden, and they walked slowly across the lawn, through the little orchard to the vegetable garden. He was impressed with the greenhouse and the rows of potatoes and seedlings, but he didn't want to linger looking at them.

"I used to pretend this slope was a mountain," said Freda. "And, Derek, I once made a fire in the bird-bath and cooked a stew over it. It tasted horrible. I think I got paraffin in it by mistake."

Somehow Freda seemed to be younger and different against this background, which was as far removed from his own life as that of a Ukrainian peasant. Had she been richer he would have been more at ease. He had seen houses with tennis courts and swimming pools when his ship's company had been entertained by various wealthy men on the Riviera and the Mediterranean. But this seemed to him to be a middle way with nothing to commend it. It wasn't a smart house, he bet they didn't have one of those cocktail cabinets even, but it wasn't easygoing and homely like his own home or her rooms at Bannerton Gardens. He wished she had stayed unattached to her past, a girl in London belonging to Jubilee Road and Kensington and himself. To have been as intimate as he had been with a girl who lived here seemed all wrong. The associations altered her. He regarded her almost with hostility.

They were almost back at the house now, and the french windows were open.

"We'll go in this way," said Freda. "I expect my father will be in the drawing-room."

She led the way in and Derek followed her nervously. Mr. Mackenzie rose from the chair in which he was reading the papers and held out a hand.

"How d'you do? Did you have a good journey?"

"This is Derek," said Freda. Derek shook the outstretched hand, but he was embarrassed and did not grasp it very firmly. Then he hastily withdrew his hand and snatched off his hat. Moving away, he found himself face to face with his reflection in a mirror edged with blue Bristol glass; it distorted slightly, but not enough to disguise the fact that in taking off his hat his carefully watered-down hair had become untidied. He certainly couldn't meet Freda's mother with his hair like that. He took a comb out of his jumper and flicked it across his head. That was better. He put the comb away again.

He had combed his hair in Freda's room countless times and she had scarcely noticed he was doing it, but here, in her family drawing-room, she felt acutely uncomfortable. She glanced at her father to see if he had noticed, but he misinterpreted her look to be one of mutual mock-horror, and raised his eyebrows with a little smile. Quickly Freda looked away, not returning her father's smile, for that would have been disloyal to Derek. Suppose he did comb his hair? she thought. Why should it matter?

"Derek," she asked him, "would you like a sherry?"

"Yes please." He was extremely formal and polite.

Freda took a decanter out of an oak corner cupboard. "Daddy?"

"Sherry?" he said. "No, I'll have a whisky."

But the choice was not put to Derek.

"Do sit down," suggested Freda.

He looked about him. Most of the chairs had loose covers of patterned green linen, and as the room had been freshly done the cushions were smooth and uncrumpled. He sat down gracelessly on the edge of a wing chair, not liking to lean back, but barely had he seated himself than Mrs. Mackenzie came in from the garden carrying a basket of vegetables.

"Oh, I didn't realize you were here," she said to Derek who was on his feet again. "How do you do? I'll just take this into the kitchen or there won't be any vegetables for lunch." She turned to her husband. "What a bloody mess you left in the toolshed, Henry! Don't you ever clean a spade?"

Derek was thoroughly shocked. Swearing and she was supposed to be a lady. He'd found it an awful strain keeping check of himself with Freda, and words only slipped out occasionally when he was angry. Why, his mother wouldn't say a thing like that in company, and she was only a working-class woman. And not even waiting to be properly introduced.

Freda was standing by the fireplace holding her sherry glass. Mrs. Mackenzie had gone, and Derek didn't know what to do. He couldn't sit down if Freda was standing, he thought. His mind clung rigidly to all the tenets of good behaviour. He stood in the middle of the floor, his feet together, holding tightly to the stem of his glass.

"Freda," said Mrs. Mackenzie, coming back into the room again and pouring herself out a drink, "why don't you take Derek up to your room and play a few records before lunch? I'm sure he'd like that. It's boring for him to sit about down here."

"Yes," said Derek, grateful for an escape. "I'd like that."

He followed Freda up the panelled stairway to her bedroom. She closed the door and put her arms round his neck.

"Derek, do relax. No one's going to eat you."

He was seized with anger by her ease and patronizing tone, but he couldn't find the words to voice it. Instead he took her arms away.

"I told you, Freda, not 'ere. Let's see what records you got."

He sat listening to them and not attempting to speak until Mrs. Mackenzie called them down to lunch.

Freda caught the glance of amusement that passed between her parents as she and Derek came into the room. It wasn't a malicious look, but simply brought about by the unusual sight of a big-boned blond sailor ambling across the parquet floor of their dining-room. She was torn again between the two worlds of her parents and Derek. She smiled at her mother, and was immediately angry at herself for giving way.

Mr. Mackenzie was standing by the sideboard, ready to carve the roast chicken waiting on the hotplate.

"What can I give you, Derek? I'm sure you're hungry."

Derek wasn't crazy about chicken. But he *was* hungry. He helped himself lavishly to potatoes and swamped them in gravy from the silver gravy-boat Freda passed him, and sprinkled it all with salt. He was on his best behaviour, because he was determined not to let Freda down. He watched carefully to see which knives the others used before he picked up his own, he spoke only when spoken to.

Why on earth doesn't he talk? thought Freda irritably. Why can't he tell them some of the anecdotes he tells me? They must think he's the most tedious boy they've ever met.

"Don't be shy, Derek," said Mrs. Mackenzie kindly, seeing him struggle to cut the meat off the bone. "Use your fingers. I'm going to." And she took the bone from her own plate between her fingers and thumb and bit off a piece of meat. "It's the only way to eat chicken."

Derek could scarcely believe his eyes and ears.

"I can manage all right, thanks," he said. What did she think he was, eating with his fingers? Where did she think he'd been brought up? He fought on doggedly with his knife and fork.

After they had eaten, he and Freda went for a walk. Having coffee had been a strain, balancing a little cup and trying not to crumple the green linen chair cover. He had formed an intense dislike for Mrs. Mackenzie, and was glad when she suggested they went out. Freda felt annoyed with Derek. As she walked along the lane beside him she thought angrily that he might at least have tried to be sociable, instead of sitting there like an oaf. He had been positively surly, while her parents had gone out of their way to be friendly. Surely he could have made some effort to respond.

She very much wanted to recapture an old mood of affection. She had planned a walk through lovely countryside, but certain he would rebuff her, she did not take his arm.

They scarcely conversed at all as they sauntered across the bumpy field into the Copse, but it was not a comfortable silence.

"I told you I didn't ought to 'ave come," said Derek suddenly. "I don't fit in, that's all there is to it."

"You could fit in perfectly well if you wanted," said Freda tartly, "only it means making an effort. You simply sat there, all through lunch, like an idiot with nothing to say for yourself."

"I suppose your mother thought she'd make me feel at 'ome," countered Derek, "by pickin' up 'er food with 'er 'ands."

"Oh," Freda shrugged hopelessly. "You're behaving like a child. For goodness' sake act normally, and stop being so sensitive."

"I thought bein' sensitive was the reason you took me up for," said Derek furiously. "You done nothin' but keep tellin' me that's what I am. Sorry I can't oblige all the time." He trod down on a fallen branch and sent the little twigs flying.

"We'd better get off the path," said Freda. "I can hear horses coming, and there's no point in being knocked down."

Round a dark green curve of fir trees, their hooves brushing through the pine needles and last year's rotting leaves, came three horses pulling at a trot.

"Why, it's Freda," called out one of the riders as they drew level. "Don't you come up to the stables any more?"

"I believe she's given us up," said the man close behind her. "Seriously, Freda, how about a ride next weekend?"

"I'll see," said Freda, smiling up at them. "Find out if there's a horse for me first. Hallo, Judy," she said, as the third rider came past.

"Hallo and goodbye," said the girl, flicking the branch overhead with her crop. "See you next week perhaps?"

The horses pulled up slightly as they reached the straight path, then broke into a gentle canter and were gone.

"That was a girl I was at school with," said Freda, hoping that the interlude had destroyed their quarrel.

"Ashamed to introduce me?" asked Derek, staring ahead.

"Oh, Derek, there wasn't time to introduce you. Please don't go on being like this, of course I wasn't ashamed." But she had been ashamed, and she had been glad the three riders had not stopped, but only called out as they passed.

As they turned back to the house for tea, Derek said in a distant voice, "I don't see there's much point in my comin' back to your flat tonight."

Freda suddenly felt as if her whole body had been anaesthetized.

"Not come back?"

"We're not exactly soul-mates, are we?" Derek said. "We might 'ave known all along it would end like this." He had had enough of the strained atmosphere, the awkwardness, the arguing.

"End?" repeated Freda in a small voice.

"Well, there don't seem much point us goin' on after this, does there?" He was sick of her moods and these continual emotional situations. He enjoyed her company, she enjoyed his, they slept together and they both enjoyed that. That was how he wanted it, simple, uncomplicated. Better to pack it in now, than drag on and on, he told himself; today had shown him that.

Freda didn't answer him. She still felt numb from the sudden shock which had punctured her self-possession like the needle of a syringe. The last night, she said to herself unbelievingly. If he'd gone away tomorrow and then not come back it wouldn't have been so bad, but to finish everything now—where had the day gone wrong? What had she done to spoil it?

She'd known how difficult it had been for him, and although he had embarrassed her and irritated her, even in those moments of irritation she had thought how sweet he was, like a bewildered puppy which she would later console with all her affection. She had looked forward to obliterating, tonight in London, the difficulties of today in the country.

They walked another hundred yards in silence, the earth soft beneath them, the smell of young bracken pungent in the afternoon sunlight.

"If that's how you feel . . ." she said at last.

They had tea in the drawing-room at a quarter past four. There were buttered biscuits spread with smoked roe, and some little currant cakes and scones.

"Did you enjoy your walk?" Mrs. Mackenzie asked them. "Which way did you go?"

"We went across to the Copse," said Freda. "We met Judy and Tony out riding with that other girl, I always forget her name."

"How is Judy?" said Mrs. Mackenzie. "We haven't seen her for a long while. Why don't you ask her in for supper one weekend?"

"I will," Freda agreed. "It's a good idea."

One weekend, any weekend now. It didn't matter.

Time seemed interminable until they left to catch the bus to the station.

"Goodbye," said Derek. "It was nice of you to 'ave me down."

"I'm glad you came," said Mrs. Mackenzie. "Perhaps another time when you're on leave you'll come again."

During the journey back to London Freda tried to talk, not about themselves, but to break down the dreadful antagonism. Derek answered her, and that was all. As they neared London she said to him almost pleadingly.

"Derek, we can't just say goodbye at Victoria, as if we'd met in a station café or something and travelled up together. Please, won't you come back, just for half an hour, and have a cup of coffee? I won't try and make you stay longer, I promise."

"Okay," he said brusquely, without looking at her, although inwardly he was grateful to her for having made the suggestion. "I'll come back for 'alf an hour."

He picked up an evening paper that someone had left on the seat and started to read the short story.

X

"Well," said Derek, "I'll be shovin' off now." He set his coffee-cup down on the low table in front of him and stood up, suddenly awkward. He foresaw the possibility of an emotional parting and he was determined to avoid it if he could. But how did one say goodbye in such circumstances? What a fool he'd been to come back here. He should have left her at Victoria.

Freda did not get up too, but stared at him from where she sat with a kind of desperation. The gas fire coughed discreetly and one bar turned blue. Freda pulled herself out of the armchair, put the fire out, waited a moment, and then relit it.

Derek moved his shoulders irritably. Why didn't she quit stalling? He'd said he was going. Well, let him go and get it over with for goodness' sake.

Freda sat back on her heels and held her hands tightly on her lap.

"Derek, please don't go yet."

"Look, Freda," he said roughly, "don't let's prolong it. It's not easy for either of us, is it?"

"But why?" she burst out. "Why are you going? What's gone wrong? I know today was a strain, and I see now I shouldn't have asked you down, but surely it can't have made such a difference. Don't you want me any more?"

"Yes," he said after a pause. "But I reckon that's all I do want."

Freda looked down at her hands, and then picked a piece of cotton off her skirt.

"I'm sorry, Freda, but you've just got to accept it. I'm not the right sort of bloke for you."

"You are, Derek," she said passionately, "you know you are. I've never been so happy as I have been these last three weeks."

"I suppose that's why you've cried when I've gone with someone else, and why we do nothin' but row," he said brutally. "It ain't my idea of bein' 'appy."

He flung himself down in the chair again.

"Freda, I'm sorry, but it just can't work. You keep tryin' to make me what I'm not. I'm all right as I am. I'm a sailor, and I got a sailor's 'abits by now. I can't be tied down like you want. It isn't that I don't like bein' with you, you know I do or I wouldn't 'ave seen you as much as I 'ave done. You're nice to be with, and you're nice sleepin' with, but . . ." He shrugged for want of words.

"Is that all I am?" she said miserably. "Nice to sleep with?"

"For Christ's sake," said Derek, "there's more to it than that. I liked the concert you took me to, and the film. I just don't want that sort of thing all the time."

"Neither do I want it all the time," said Freda. "I want you."

She stood up and walked over to the window. "Derek, I do see your point of view. I know I was wrong. Your mother doesn't like me, and my mother wouldn't think you were suitable for me if she knew about us. But let's keep our families out of it. I want you on any terms. I don't want it to end."

She had her back to him, but he knew her eyes were full of tears.

"No," he said stubbornly, "there's no point in talkin' about terms. You don't like my 'ome, and I don't like yours. And you can't take me for what I am, just like at Pompey last Monday."

Let her have it, he thought unkindly, and then he could go.

"Just because we'd 'ad a few in the Compasses, you 'ad to start naggin' at me. Then the next thing I knows you'd pushed off 'ome. Well, 'ow do you think I felt? I was miserable as sin, and got so bloody drunk the cops nabbed me and I spent the night in clink, and got fined practically all the money I'd got. If you 'ad your way I'd be sittin' in Kensington Gardens sippin' lemonade. Well, that ain't what I want, see."

Freda suddenly turned round to face him, and he saw that tears were pouring down her face.

"Don't start cryin' again," he shouted. "I can't stand it." He felt helpless now as well as angry. He went over to her and put his hands on her shoulders. "Look, Freda, pack it in, will you? It won't do no good."

She put her head down on his chest, weeping.

"Oh, Derek. I couldn't bear it if I didn't see you again."

Her tears were soaking into his vest, her head seemed to be loose, like a doll's. Why didn't she make an effort to control herself instead of clinging to him? His rage mounted, he would like to have shaken her.

Without intending to, he kissed her on the forehead.

"Freda, don't keep on cryin'." He jerked her shoulders back so that her face was upturned and kissed her hard on the mouth. Her cheeks felt wet and burning against his. He did shake her now.

"Stop cryin', for Christ's sake."

Her arms went round him and held him.

"Derek, you mustn't leave me."

He pulled her arms away and grasped her by the wrists. He didn't want anything more to do with her. He was going, and quick. He loosened his grip and started to move away. Freda stood still, making no effort to stop him.

Almost hating her, and despising himself, he turned suddenly and kissed her with all his force.

They had drawn back the curtains and lay in the pale light that came through the open window.

"Derek?" Freda asked him, "would you like to have a photograph of me?"

"Yes. All right." His arm had gone to sleep and he moved away from her, rubbing it with his free hand.

"Shall I give it to you now or tomorrow?"

"I'm goin' to Pompey tomorrow," he said.

"I know, but not till late. Still, I'll try and find it now, I think."

She got out of bed and went over to her bureau desk, pulled down the top and rummaged in the pigeonholes, bringing out bundles of letters, and finally an orange snapshot folder. She proceeded to hold the photographs up to the light, one at a time, then scrutinized them closely.

Derek watched her moodily. Tomorrow! he thought. He supposed she imagined tomorrow they'd spend the day in bed. He hoisted himself on his elbows, turned the pillow over and banged it. Then he pressed his face against the cool linen.

"Here it is." Freda came back and climbed on to the bed beside him. "It's not very like me, but it's the only one I've got of me alone. My father took it on my last day at college."

"Thanks." Derek took the snapshot and put it on the bedside table. "I'll look at it properly in the mornin'." He kissed her on the side of her mouth. "I'm tired as 'ell, Freda. Let's get some sleep."

He turned over and put his head down on his arm, and assumed deep, slow breathing. He was aware that Freda had not moved, and was probably lying uncomfortably, even cold, because she thought he was asleep and did not want to disturb him.

Freda sleepily stretched out her hand and felt on the table for Derek's watch. Her fingers found the metal base of the bedside lamp, then the corner of a paperbacked book, then the cold smooth china of a cup. She was immediately awake. Derek? But he wasn't beside her, and she saw that the covers had been carefully tucked against her own body, so that the part of the bed where he had been wasn't covered, and all that was there was the bottom sheet, crumpled and ridged.

She sat up, with the thought that he was either in the kitchenette or the bathroom, but the doors of both were open. She looked at the chair, and his uniform, which he always folded swiftly and carefully even in moments of considerable passion, was gone.

Her eyes came back to the yellow cup by the bed. In it the tea was cold, the milk a grey scum on the surface. The smell of it suddenly reached her nostrils, and she pushed the cup away from her as far as she could, and lay back on the pillow.

He'd gone. How long ago? How could she have slept through it? He must have been very quiet. She had a half-memory now of him leaving the bed, but she had been too nearly asleep to realize. Or perhaps she only thought she remembered. Curiously, she did not want to cry.

She got up quickly, and made the bed so that the sheets were taut and all trace that Derek had slept there was gone. She poured the cold tea down the sink. His own cup, washed but not dried, was upside down on the draining board, the saucer balanced against it.

Freda put on the kettle and made a pot of tea. She sat huddled by her gas fire, drinking it. I must get out, she thought, I can't stand this. She looked at the clock and saw that it had only just gone seven. Seven on a Sunday morning—her one day of getting up late!

She dressed but didn't make up, slightly enjoying the sight of her pale face in the mirror, the black smudges under her eyes.

She walked along Gloucester Road, then turned up towards Prince's Gate. There was no one else about except an old man with a brown moustache who trundled a dustcart down the centre of the road. The shops were deserted, the houses, too, seemed to have been abandoned. Impossible at this moment to believe that in each one, in the hundreds of bed-sitting-rooms, girls like herself were sleeping, without having to awaken to the bleak realization that their lovers had gone. She had a mental picture of Derek again, his suntanned shoulders, his fair hair above the sheets. It was incredible that an emotion she knew had never been love could be so overwhelming. Would he ever come back? It seemed unfair that she had known him for so short a time. What good has it done? she asked herself. I've lost Matthew, I've got no one. Derek had awakened in her a latent sensuality, and losing him left her with an aching unfulfilment, an over-abundance of affection with no one on whom to lavish it. Nothing to look forward to but school, with a class she couldn't control, and Derek's sister in front of her every single day. It's true that affairs only make women unhappy, she thought, not only from a moral point of view, but from an emotional one.

Freda had always maintained that immorality was not so much whether you did or did not sleep with someone, but in your psychological attitude to the person with whom you slept. If she gave herself to someone purely to satisfy her sexual longing, she felt that that was immoral. But if she did it because it was the ultimate, most personal thing she had to offer in a relationship, she felt it was both morally and spiritually permissible.

Derek had been her first real affair. Walking now through the depressing Sunday morning streets, she realized that her philosophy of love, often expressed in those very terms during her last year at the university, was an illusion as thin and ineffectual as a threadbare coat.

This is literally the cold grey light of dawn, she thought to herself, as behind her, over the Albert Hall, the sun rose like a small dinner gong, varnishing the leaves in the park, and reflecting in odd windows of offices and shops. In front of her Kensington High Street curved away towards Derry and Toms, the grey pavements like the blades of twin sickles.

Freda turned back to Bannerton Gardens. She felt too tired to walk further. Crying and not much sleep had combined to exhaust her.

As she climbed the stairs, the door of Mrs. Gibson-Brown's flat opened.

"Oh, Miss Mackenzie, it's you. I'd like a word with you."

"What, now?" asked Freda.

"I didn't expect to see you until Monday, Miss Mackenzie."

"No," said Freda wearily, "I came back on Saturday this time."

She followed the kimonoed figure of Mrs. Gibson-Brown into the *salon*, which had not yet been cleaned from yesterday. Dead ashes were in the grate, and a gold-fluted coffee-cup stood on the floor by an armchair, the unstirred sugar crystallized at the bottom.

"I really can't have strange men coming into the house," began Mrs. Gibson-Brown, clasping the kimono over her stomach. "I was most surprised to find that sailor in your room on Friday morning, Miss Mackenzie."

"I know," Freda said. "He told me."

"He was extremely insolent to me," said Mrs. Gibson-Brown haughtily. "Miss Mackenzie, I must tell you now that if you let him continue to come here at these odd hours, I shall have to ask you to leave."

"You needn't worry," said Freda, turning to go. "I don't suppose he'll be here again."

"I don't want to seem unreasonable," persisted Mrs. Gibson-Brown. "But you know the conditions on which I let my flatlets. And you must admit, Miss Mackenzie, I've waived my rules very freely for you, in respect to Mr. Taylor."

"Yes," agreed Freda, "you've been most kind. Now if you don't mind, Mrs. Gibson-Brown, I'll go upstairs. I'm rather tired, and I have a lot of work to do today."

"If you'd like the *Sunday Times* later," Mrs. Gibson-Brown called after her in a friendly tone, as Freda unlocked her front door, "don't hesitate to ask me for it."

"Thank you," answered Freda from the landing. "I shan't have much time for reading the Sunday papers."

She entered her room, took off her coat, and lit the fire. Then picking up a pencil she sat down on the bed and began marking the pile of green history notebooks.

XI

Derek had left on an impulse. He had woken up and looked at Freda lying beside him, and he had wanted to make love to her. Not again, he said to himself. This time I'm going. He slid out from under the bedclothes and arranged them so that Freda should not feel the draught. Then he crept across the room on his naked feet and put the kettle on the stove to boil while he dressed. He dropped his shoe and Freda stirred. He held his breath, but she didn't wake. The kettle whistled slightly and the steam puffed once or twice and then expelled itself in a steady stream. One shoe on, one shoe off, he made tea and leaned against the sink, drinking. Then he poured out a cup for Freda and tiptoed over to put it by the bed. Beside his watch lay the snapshot she had given him last night. He put it carefully inside his paybook, finished dressing, combed his hair, and left the flat.

As the door latched behind him the feeling of freedom and relief was surprising.

He had walked as far as the Albert Memorial when a lone car pulled up and offered him a lift.

"Thanks," said Derek. "Don't mind if I do."

They sped along the road, the still closed park on one side of them, the crescents of shuttered homes on the other, past the grey islands of Hyde Park Corner, and down towards Piccadilly.

"Up early," commented the driver. "Which way are you heading?"

"Mile End," answered Derek.

"I'll take you on a bit," said the man. "You won't find transport at this hour."

Derek was pleased, although he did not consider the stranger's goodwill particularly remarkable. He put it down to his uniform. He had left Bannerton Gardens at half-past five on a Sunday morning, with a considerable distance to travel, yet not once had it presented itself to him as a difficulty. He merely wanted to be out of the flat by the time Freda woke and started another scene. He hadn't really thought about getting a lift, but it did not surprise him when the car drew up. It was the way of the world. One got home somehow.

The driver stopped outside Liverpool Street Station.

"This any good to you?"

"Thanks," said Derek. "It'll do nicely. It ain't far from 'ere. So long." He stepped on to the pavement, slammed the door, and with his arms directed the man as he turned the car in the middle of the empty street. Then he gave a half-wave, half-salute, and swung off in the direction of Jubilee Road.

At ten to seven he was home. It was Sunday, and his family

wouldn't be up for hours. He went upstairs quietly, holding his shoes in his hand, into the room where Joan still slept. His own bed was in the corner, behind a brown canvas screen. It creaked as he climbed into it, and Joan sat up.

"Derry?"

"Yeah?"

"Where you been?"

"Oh, go to sleep." He turned over and pulled the blanket up to his ears. Joan sighed and lay down again. The sun rose and shone through the thin curtains on to her make-up bottles on the table under the window. The film of face powder on the lids was suddenly visible.

"Derry?"

He didn't answer.

"Derry?"

After a moment Joan gave it up and attempted to go back to sleep.

Joan brought him his breakfast.

"You didn't 'alf get in late," she said, sitting on the foot of his bed and cramping his feet.

Derek ate his fried egg. "So what?" he asked. "See 'ere, Joan," he added after a second, "if Mum asks you what time I come in, say you was asleep. I'm sick of 'er askin' questions like I was a kid."

"Okay," Joan giggled. "Derry, was you out with Miss Mackenzie?"

"No, I told you, I went to the country, and I 'ad to 'itch back." He put down his plate. "Now beat it, Joanie. I'm goin' to get up."

She gave him an almost flirtatious look and went over to her jars of make-up, and selected a bottle of nail-varnish.

"I'm goin' to do me nails. This is more my room than yours."

She poured some acetone on to a piece of cottonwool and the smell of it spread across the room.

"I said beat it," ordered Derek truculently.

"Derry, is it true 'bout you and Miss Mackenzie?"

"Is what true?" Derek demanded. "You get out of 'ere, Joan Smith, before I 'as to throw you."

She giggled again, and walked slowly to the door. "I bet it is true." Her voice reached him again from the stairs, goading him. " 'Er name's Freda, ain't it, Derry?"

He dressed and went down to the kitchen. His father had already been out and brought back the Sunday papers. He was now absorbed, studying form.

Derek sat down opposite him.

"Give us a paper, Dad."

Mrs. Smith came in from the yard, and started to peel the potatoes for dinner. Joan perched on the table near Derek, and drew the clogged brush smudgily over her nails.

" 'Strewth," said Derek, holding his nose. "That smell!"

He and his father went down to the William Tell at half-past eleven.

"Goin' back tonight," Derek said (it seemed to him a thousand times) in answer to the enquiries from the morning regulars. He beat his father at darts, had four pints, and the two of them walked home happily, a little late for dinner.

"You goin' up to say goodbye to Maureen?" asked Mrs. Smith as she dished out the treacle pudding.

"No," said Derek. "What the 'ell for?"

Joan sniggered delightedly.

"Miss Mackenzie's 'is girl now."

Derek looked at her furiously. "I ain't got a girl," he said coldly, scraping up the golden syrup with his fork.

Johnnie turned up at half-past three, disturbing the family rest.

"I was that chokka," he explained, "I thought we might as well get back for somethin' to do."

"Yeah!" Derek, who had been dozing in the steamy kitchen, was already halfway to the door. "Give us a minute to get me gear."

He flung his belongings into his case, suddenly animated by the thought of returning to *Dragon*. He hurried downstairs again, with scarcely time for his farewells.

His parents and Joan stood in a little group by the table.

" 'Bye, Mum, I'm off." He kissed her perfunctorily. "So long,

Dad, be good, Joanie." His eyes shone. "Okay, Johnnie, let's go. What time's the train?"

"I reckoned we'd get one 'bout 'alf-past four."

"Let's 'ave a wet before we go. Got any beer, Dad?"

There was a half-empty bottle on the dresser. Derek divided it carefully into two glasses, for the first time slowing up his actions since Johnnie's arrival. They drained them in a second.

"Be seein' you," said Derek. This departure certainly wasn't emotional. "'Bye, all."

"'Bye, all," echoed Johnnie's voice from the front door. It slammed loudly. They walked down the path.

"Blimey," said Derek, "there's the bus."

He and Johnnie set off at a run along the narrow pavement of Jubilee Road, and hurled themselves on to the platform a second before the automatic doors closed.

They put their cases in the small hold, and took out their money.

"Two to Mile End," said Derek, winking at the clippie.

XII

Fauntleroy was at the barrier with his mother.

"Why," cried out Mrs. McEwan in a voice which carried powerfully, "isn't that the young man we met at the concert?"

"Where?" Fauntleroy looked round and saw Johnnie and Derek approaching from the Waterloo Road subway. They walked slightly apart, dodging porters and mail trucks.

"Ain't it smashin'," said Johnnie, "tomorrow we 'as our tot again."

A wonderful tot-assured future stretched before him. It gave point to life, it was a landmark in his day.

"Look out!" warned Derek suddenly. "There's old Faunty with 'is mother. Quick, I'm goin' to 'ide meself in the 'eads." He looked round frantically for the sign saying 'Gentlemen'.

But it was too late. The words "at the concert" floated distinctly to his ears. Mrs. McEwan waved a gloved hand.

"Hallo!"

Derek walked over to her resignedly, Johnnie close behind him.

" 'Afternoon," he said. He remembered his manners. "This is my oppo, Johnnie Cooper."

"Good afternoon, Cooper," said Mrs. McEwan smiling, and extending the gloved hand.

Johnnie shook it gingerly and muttered a greeting.

"Been to any more concerts, Smith?" asked Fauntleroy, politely making conversation. He would have liked to have had these last few moments with his mother alone.

Derek glanced swiftly at Johnnie and shook his head.

" 'E loves classical music," said Johnnie jeeringly. "Spent 'alf 'is leave in the Albert 'All."

"Now then," said Mrs. McEwan. "I call that very unfair. We met Smith at the Festival Hall with a charming young lady."

Derek glared at her.

" 'Oo was that?" Johnnie demanded. "Freda? Or 'ave you been 'oldin' out on me. Don't know as 'ow I'd call 'er charmin'."

Mrs. McEwan met her son's eye. You poor boy, her glance conveyed. Are these really the sort of people you have to mix with?

"You're 'ere early, ain't you?" said Derek to Fauntleroy. "In an 'urry to get back?"

"Michael hates having to rush," Mrs. McEwan answered for him. "He'd far rather get back to his ship with time to unpack his things in comfort."

Derek and Johnnie looked at one another and grinned. That would go down well on the mess-deck.

"We'd better go and find a seat," said Derek. "I don't go much on standin' all the way. Be seein' you."

"Goodbye," said Mrs. McEwan. "I hope you have a pleasant journey back."

He and Johnnie showed their travel warrants, almost coming apart where they had been folded for an entire leave.

"Keep a place for me," Fauntleroy called after them.

"Blimey," said Johnnie. "Fancy 'avin' an old woman like that."

They found a compartment and Johnnie flopped down on the seat.

"I'm goin' to get my 'ead down," he announced. "Wake me up

when we gets there." He tipped his hat over his eyes and made a comic face.

Derek roared with laughter.

"You ain't changed," he said happily.

He put his head out of the window and watched Fauntleroy threading his way along the platform, peering anxiously into each compartment looking for them.

"Faunty," he shouted, "we're in 'ere."

Fauntleroy looked relieved and climbed into the train. On his left cheek, just below his eye, was a pale smudge of lipstick.

"Your Mum's been 'avin' a go at you," observed Johnnie. "Take a dekko at yourself, mate."

Fauntleroy examined himself in the mirror, then, blushing slightly, spat on to his handkerchief and rubbed the mark away.

"I met a smashin' bint last night," said Johnnie, the lipstick on the handkerchief having started a train of reminiscences. "Picked 'er up down Islington. Black 'air. Colour of tar." He was quite poetic. "You got a party, Faunty?"

It had been a popular bait on *Dragon's* last trip.

"I know several girls," answered Fauntleroy temperately. "I don't have anyone in particular."

"Don't suppose your Mum'd welcome one, eh, Faunty?" suggested Johnnie.

"Oh, put a sock in it." Derek thought Johnnie was going a bit far. "We can't all 'ave your sex-appeal."

The whistle blew, and the train moved away from the platform, gathering speed.

They stared out of the windows.

"It doesn't seem like three weeks, does it?" said Fauntleroy, taking a copy of the *Listener* out of his case.

"It seems a bloody sight longer than that to me," answered Johnnie.

"I expect you chaps are broke by now," said Fauntleroy. "Let me buy you both a pint."

"Thanks," said Johnnie, warming to him. "Won't say no, will we, Smudge?"

With unhurried step the three of them turned from the station towards the Compasses, carrying their cases.

"Wonder 'ow long we'll be on *Dragon*?" ruminated Derek, taking a gulp of his black and tan.

"I fully expect to be washing up at the barracks next week," said Fauntleroy. "Personally I shouldn't mind. I'd give anything to get home more often."

"I could go a couple of years in the Middle East, meself," said Johnnie dreamily. "The things they tell you about the women. France ain't in it."

"Same again," said Fauntleroy to the barmaid.

"We'll pay you back when it ain't blank week," Derek promised. "I needed this somethin' chronic. 'Aven't 'ad a drop since before dinner, bar that little sip at my 'ome."

They put down their glasses and pushed their way through the crowd of sailors to the door. They walked more hurriedly now, down towards the dockyard.

" 'Ome sweet 'ome," said Johnnie grinning, as they went through the gate, exchanging the usual ribald remarks with the man on duty.

They walked on past the dockyard buildings, so many of which seemed temporary structures, nissen huts, and sheds made of corrugated asbestos, which had been hastily put up in the war and somehow never replaced by anything more permanent.

They turned the corner, and there was *Dragon*, looking as if she had not moved since they left her three weeks ago. Here and there her pale grey hull and upperworks were marked with irregular blotches of red lead, like the dapplings of a forest animal. A thin wisp of smoke freed itself from the for'ard funnel. The radar antennae were silhouetted against the evening sky like an elaborate mobile.

Derek led the way up the makeshift gangway, on to the familiar steel deck, feeling the rivets and ridges of her plates through the soles of his shoes. The three of them moved aft, and down to the noisy mess-deck, where a radio played Family Favourites at full blast.

Derek, Johnnie and Faunty quickly commandeered three vacant

lockers, and slung their hammocks, so that they were strategically placed for access to the heads and the movable blowers of the air-conditioning system.

Faunty unpacked his things and arranged them slowly and methodically in his locker, the neat pile of socks and underwear topped by the leather toilet-case. By contrast, Johnnie slung his belongings into his locker haphazardly.

"Flogged a pair of shoes, yesterday, Smudge," he said. "Reckon I won't 'ave any pay due for the 'ole of this trip, what with Mum's allotment, and 'alf me gear gone."

"Yeah, I was thinkin' of pawnin' me raincoat," said Derek, "but it ain't worth it. The bloke only offered me ten bob, so I told 'im what 'e could do with it."

Lying in his hammock he watched Johnnie sticking a large coloured pin-up of a Hollywood film star on the inside of his locker door.

"I'd swop 'er for the Chief Petty Officer any day," remarked Derek.

"Give 'im a couple of falsies and 'e wouldn't be so bad," rejoined Johnnie, pressing down the Sellotape firmly with his thumb.

The exaggerated curves of the pin-up made Derek think of Freda and the photograph she had given him. He took it out of the inside of his jumper and looked at it, wondering if he should put it up in place of his usual collection of cover girls.

Freda stood almost to attention on a flight of stone steps. She looked younger than he remembered her, and a little self-conscious. Her hair was done differently, and her plain, high-necked dress and flat-heeled shoes made her seem shorter and fatter than she was. She couldn't compete with a Hollywood star.

With a quick movement he tore the photograph into small pieces. Holding them in his fist, he swung himself out of his hammock and dropped on to the deck. He picked his way across the mess and stood up on the wooden bench that ran along the side of the sloping bulkhead. With his right hand he reached up and unscrewed the heavy bolt securing the metal cover of the port, pulling it back to open the port itself. He thrust his hand through the porthole, and let the pieces drop. He didn't look but he could imagine them falling into the dark oily water between the ship and the dockside. Then he closed the port again with a clang, and screwed the bolt back into place, watching the spirals of the polished brass thread as he did so.

ALSO AVAILABLE FROM VALANCOURT BOOKS

MICHAEL ARLEN	Hell! said the Duchess
R. C. ASHBY (RUBY FERGUSON)	He Arrived at Dusk
FRANK BAKER	The Birds
CHARLES BEAUMONT	The Hunger and Other Stories
DAVID BENEDICTUS	The Fourth of June
CHARLES BIRKIN	The Smell of Evil
JOHN BLACKBURN	A Scent of New-Mown Hay
	Broken Boy
	Blue Octavo
	The Flame and the Wind
	Nothing but the Night
	Bury Him Darkly
	The Face of the Lion
THOMAS BLACKBURN	The Feast of the Wolf
JOHN BRAINE	Room at the Top
	The Vodi
R. CHETWYND-HAYES	The Monster Club
BASIL COPPER	The Great White Space
	Necropolis
HUNTER DAVIES	Body Charge
JENNIFER DAWSON	The Ha-Ha
BARRY ENGLAND	Figures in a Landscape
RONALD FRASER	Flower Phantoms
GILLIAN FREEMAN	The Leather Boys
	The Leader
STEPHEN GILBERT	Bombardier
	Monkeyface
	The Burnaby Experiments
	Ratman's Notebooks
MARTYN GOFF	The Youngest Director
STEPHEN GREGORY	The Cormorant
THOMAS HINDE	Mr. Nicholas
	The Day the Call Came
CLAUDE HOUGHTON	I Am Jonathan Scrivener
	This Was Ivor Trent
GERALD KERSH	Nightshade and Damnations
	Fowlers End
FRANCIS KING	Never Again
	An Air That Kills
	The Dividing Stream
	The Dark Glasses

Lightning Source UK Ltd.
Milton Keynes UK
UKOW05f0156030114

223869UK00002B/24/P